MW01064505

Merry Chris

Witch

Ek Dawn

Happy Reading!!

This one's for my mom. May the echoes of winter cheer surround you throughout the year. I love you.

Copyright © 2015 by CK Dawn

All rights reserved.

Merry Chris Witch is a work of fiction. Names, characters, places, and incidents either are the product of the author's imagination or are used fictitiously, and any resemblance to actual persons, living or dead, events, or locales is entirely coincidental. The author recognizes the trademarks and copyrights of all registered products mentioned within this work.

No part of this publication may be reproduced, distributed, or transmitted in any form or by any means, including photocopying, recording, or other electronic or mechanical methods, without the prior written permission of the author, except in the case of brief quotations embodied in critical reviews and certain other noncommercial uses permitted by copyright law.

ISBN-13: 978-1535428910

ISBN-10: 1535428910

Editor: Celine Fowler

Cover Art by Karri Klawiter

WWW.ARTBYKARRI.COM

'Twas the night before Christmas,

and all through the realms

Magic creatures were stirring, all feeling overwhelmed;

Stockings were hung, there was no time to spare.

But St. Nicholas fell ill and wouldn't be there;

Children were nestled and slept unaware;

That Christmas was cancelled while elves felt despair.

I'm only a witch what could I possibly do?

Except try and save Christmas along beside you;

We traveled the world making such a clatter,

But I was with you so nothing else mattered.

Away to the first house we flew like a flash,

And tore the tree down creating a loud crash.

We soon got our rhythm in the fresh fallen snow,

Delivering presents to the unsuspecting below,

Name after name on the Nice List disappeared.

As we traveled the world sharing our holiday cheer.

I'll let you in on a privy if you listen quick,

She may not be Santa, but her name is still Nick;

To learn her tale you'll have to turn the page,

And weather the storm that comes with her age;

As my homage to Clement Moore comes to a close,

I hope my love for the holiday truly does show,

For a witch I may be and magic where I dwell--

But I wish you a Merry Christmas and a fare-thee-well.

Magic is real and dreams do come true.

Be careful what you Witch for.

Table of Contents

Bah Humbug

"Chris, get up! It's time for school," mom shouted to my closed door. "Don't make me tell you again!" I could hear her aggravated footsteps as she headed to the kitchen. Her irritation with me was amplified by the loud cabinet door slams and huffs under her breath.

"Ugh, but it's too cold," I moaned. *Ugh! And too close to Christmas!* My parents kept our house too chilly in the winter months for my taste, but I started to wake up anyway. I knew not to push my luck with my mom. Being cold first thing in the morning sucked, but that wasn't it, not really. I hated the holiday season more. All the red, white, and green decorations everywhere made me want to hurl.

Throwing the covers off I stumbled out of bed and made my way down the hall to the bathroom to pee. Without giving it a glance or a thought, I waived my hand towards my bedroom on the way. My rumpled comforter uncurled itself and re-covered the flat and fitted sheets. The pillows sat up against my headboard and plumped themselves. My clothes from the day before floated through the air and into the hamper, and my shoes walked themselves into my closet. Everything was tidy again, just the way mom liked it, and without me having to lift a finger. Well a wave of my hand and five fingers, but who's counting?

"Christopher Aspen Heron! Did you just use magic to make your bed?" My mom's voice scolded from the kitchen.

Crap! What was I thinking? "No," I lied, coming to a stop in the hallway and trying not to pee myself.

"Well, *I'm* not making buttercream frosting in here. I can smell your casting all the way in in this kitchen, young man! Do you want to get kicked out of this school too? No underage magic in the human world means NO underage magic in the human world, period! Not even here in the house. Do you hear me?"

"Sorry, mom," I said, rushing into the bathroom. Closing the door, I rolled my eyes, half from emptying my bladder and half for being so careless and using magic outside of school. I flushed and looked at myself in the mirror. *That was stupid, Chris, but man do I need a haircut.* My shaggy light brown curls were down to my eyelashes almost covering my hazel eyes and bordering on what girls liked to call cute. *Ugh! I hate that word.* Best to have mom trim me up, but not today. Instead, I grabbed my favorite New York Yankees baseball cap and threw it on. It had been a souvenir from my dad after going to our first human baseball game together when I was a kid right after our move to the city. A time before I had come into my powers and a time before I kept getting myself into trouble with said powers.

I threw my clothes on in a hurry. Today I wanted to get out of the house as fast as possible after my relapse of magic use. Mom and Dad had always been pretty loose with the no underage magic rule around the house once I came into my powers. That was until I went and screwed everything up on Halloween. It sucked not being able to use my powers in the privacy of our house anymore, but I guess that was part of my punishment and I'd just have to deal. Brushing my hand down my jaw I shook my head. *Can't stay in here all day and avoid the inevitable.* I could already hear the lecture that was coming. *'Nothing good comes from always taking the easy way out, Chris. You may have come into your powers early but magic isn't a toy. That's why there are rules in place. Honestly, young man, you keep this up and you're well on your way to having your powers stripped and being forced to attend human school!'*

Ugh! I argued with myself. I thought being expelled from coven private school the day after Halloween had been the worst day of my life. I was wrong. The day I started magic public school six weeks ago had been much, much worse. I was the only witch surrounded by elves, fairies, trolls, and every magical creature imaginable all hyped up on Christmas cheer. Virtually all of them were gearing up for the Christmas season too. Elves proudly helped their parents make toys, fairies conjured more pixie dust than the reindeer could ever use to fly in ten lifetimes. Trolls were brushing up on their merry mischief making. Even mermaids were getting in on the holiday cheer, singing their cheerful songs. And then there was me, an out of place witch that hated Christmas. Okay, maybe hate was too strong a word, but I was at least allergic to it.

I was in a mood. The man in the red suit had infringed on my Halloween parade and it had been getting worse every day since. Christmas sucked and the decorations always came out too soon. Every year, just as soon as the weather got cooler, stores put out Christmas junk with barely a mention of Halloween, my favorite holiday, like ever! Does Christmas really need three months to celebrate? I mean, like really? Come on! And when they do put out Halloween stuff it's so sickening sweet and cutesy that I want to vomit. I mean what guy in his right mind wants to wear a pointed witch's hat and carry a broom or worse yet, pretend we're glittery vampires? Can we say, lame? So, I had conjured myself a ghastly costume that was sure to win the contest of this human party I had heard about. I figured I might also get some swoons from the ladies. Once I was at the party, I may have even accidentally on purpose slowed time, but only a little, just to make the party last a little bit longer. What can I say? My costume had been a hit and I was getting attention from some major hotties, I wasn't ready for the fun to end.

I thought I was so smart and had everything all figured out. No one at the party should have been able to detect my tiny use of magic. I hadn't expected the Reagent of all the covens to be at the party mingling with humans and he hadn't expected any underage witches to be using magic that powerful in their presence. Without even a glint of a warning my punishment was handed down and carried out swiftly. Immediate expulsion from coven private school and probationary enrolment in public school for magical beings. And why did my spells have to smell like butter cream frosting anyway? Why couldn't I have gotten something cool like Lynne Monty had gotten? She got winter pine and I smell like cupcakes! I swear the powers that be swapped them just for shits and giggles. Hell, I would have even settled for the fudge brownie smell like the guy from the T.V. show Warehouse Thirteen used to vibe on. Now that would have been cool! But, I guess it didn't matter in the long run. Spell smells were like acne in teenagers, mature a bit and they go away, or so my parents told me. Well that couldn't come fast enough. I was over the acne and frosting. And all the holiday cheer made me want to ho-ho-hurl. The only thing good about the holiday season if you asked me? Christmas day happened to be my birthday.

*

In the end the lecture from mom hadn't been too bad, stern looks mostly. She was probably going to wait for my dad to have a long talk with me. I rolled my eyes as I jumped off the cold New York streets and down the steps to the subway station. A few snowflakes fell from the sky and were carried on the wind currents by all the humans bustling around me. One of the snowflakes landed on my nose and melted. I could have sworn it had the faint but lingering scent of sweet peppermint. Being a witch and having some pretty powerful nature elementals on mom's side of the family, I knew that sometimes a change in the weather meant something magical was taking place. I wondered if it meant the rumors were true. I'd heard that Santa Claus' son Kris Kringle Jr, the golden boy as I liked to call him, was going to grace us with his presence at school today and boost morale. As if the elves had any emotion besides cheer and needed a pick-me-up! I swear they had eggnog running through their veins and showered in sugar sprinkles using peppermint pep shampoo.

I pulled my subway card from my pocket as I neared the gates. Its golden flecks shimmered, just like the air of the magic realm. I never tired of seeing the two worlds merge at hubs like the subway station. Humans going about their daily lives, traveling to and from work, and oblivious to the magical world all around them. I gave a little chuckle wondering if humans ever thought it curious that at least two ticket turnstiles in every train and subway station all over the world never worked and were continuously 'out of order.'

"Hey, Sam, how's life treating you?" I tossed some quarters into his metal donation cup. Sam was in his usual spot sitting up against the tile wall as heavy pedestrian traffic passed by. He called it prime real-estate for a vagabond like himself.

"Hey ya, Yankee Chris, how you doing today?"

"Can't complain. Oh, they're having a sale at your favorite deli down the street," I offered.

"Oh, oh, thanks for that." Sam tipped his cup to me, "And for these, as usual."

"See you tomorrow, Sam?"

"Of course, of course. See ya tomorrow, Yankee Chris, and Merry Christmas!"

I cringed but waved as I passed. I knew Sam meant well with his holiday cheer, but still. *Just, ugh! Stupid, Christmas.*

As I headed toward the out of order turnstiles the edges of the human world began to shimmer and shift, and just like that, I was enveloped by the magic realm where everything glowed in a golden light. Just as soon as I had been seen entering the area, humans forgot me that much quicker as I phased out of their world undetected and became part of the invisible magic realm.

Sam dumped the quarters into his hand and looked around wondering where they had come from. Later he would vaguely remember talking to me, maybe even remember me giving him the change, but he wouldn't remember that I disappeared into thin air. No one would. Scratching his head, Sam put the quarters in the pocket of his green and red flannel shirt, and greeted another person he knew.

Human sounds muffled and mortal men and women became transparent as fairies and sprites buzzed by sometimes flying right through an unknowing human or two. I spotted three of my friends from coven school and waved. They waved back sadly as they went through the first turnstile and awaited the subway to my old school. They weren't allowed to talk to me, not really. That hadn't been part of my official punishment, but coven parents were a protective bunch. They didn't want my bad influence rubbing off on their kids I suppose.

My heart started beating faster as I veered away from the second turnstile and headed to the wrong gate intentionally, straight toward the first gate that would take me to my old school. I hadn't planned on playing hooky, but I wanted to see my friends and--

Something tiny with immense strength grabbed my collar and nearly lifted me off the ground as it pulled me back to the second turnstile. *Crap!* I knew I was in trouble.

"Chris Heron, I hope you weren't thinking of skipping my class today?" A voice incongruent with the gossamer appearance of this small creature boomed and echoed off the walls of our underground station. Tiny wings beat the air like a hummingbird in flight, but this fairy had the strength of the Hulk, if he were actually real of course. Her miniature frame and white ethereal glow stood in direct opposition of the force of nature she truly was. I recognized who she was by her strength even before she had buzzed by my head and scoffed.

"No, Miss Bell," I lied.

"Good!" And with that she flew ahead of me into the terminal. Several young fairies said their hellos to her on their way to work and magic school.

"Good morning, Miss Bell," a teacher greeted her.

"Hiya, Tink," said one of the fairies in charge of harvesting pixie dust.

Yep, Tinker Bell was a real life fairy and she'd been around for a long time. She wouldn't admit to it now but she had been known to conjure and use magic in the human world when she was younger too. A human had actually even written stories about her. But I knew not to get her started on the movies and cartoons, not if I wanted to live to see my next birthday. Now she taught Environmental Conservation and Conjuring at public school for the magically gifted and was also my new principal.

I passed my golden subway card over the scanner of the second turnstile Miss Bell had directed me to and entered the station. Just out of phase, my friends' navy uniforms disappeared into a sea of coven blues as they all got on the subway car destined for my old private school. The doors swished closed and the yellow seal representing all the covens served as a stop sign on the doors, blocking my entrance. *Okay, I get it already. I'm not welcome.* I waved goodbye to my friends and waited for the next subway car that unfortunately wouldn't be out of phase. As if it heard me, my car rolled through the terminal and occupied the same space as the covens' before it started to move and left the station. It was surreal watching the two subway trains occupy the same space momentarily. They represented my two worlds. One that rejected me and the other I couldn't wait to get out of. A heavy rock felt like it had dropped into the pit of my stomach as I wondered if I'd ever be allowed back into school with the rest of the witches.

Entering the subway car destined for magic school I took a seat and tried to tune out everyone's Christmas cheer that seemed to have me surrounded. The car finally took off like a bullet down the track giving me a welcome distraction. We emerged from the dark tunnel into the golden light of the magic realm. Fields of flowers in every color imaginable blanketed the ground for miles around. Giant yellow sunflowers were tracking the sun and pink morning glories were yawning and stretching. Fairies were flying above the giant petals, harvesting the pollen for pixie dust and potion production. Magic realm cell towers floated above the fields here and there ensuring reception for our phones no matter what realm we were in.

Just then Mom texted, hoping I would have a good day at school. I knew she was worried about me. She knew I was having a rough go of it these past few weeks. She even wrote that she was making my favorite for dinner tonight, chicken spaghetti. My stomach grumbled, but even chicken spaghetti wasn't enough to cheer me up. I winced as I watched the coven train veer to the right up into the mountains toward my old school as my train headed down towards a dark damp tunnel. The tall purple and blue spires of the school followed the mountain's silhouette seamlessly. The tallest peak was one of my favorite places to hang out with my friends. We'd sit up in the old library for hours thinking up new potions and spells to try. But the mountain and my old school disappeared as we entered the bleak tunnel.

With a loud thud the troll car attached as we continued on to school without even having to stop. The doors connecting the two cars swooshed open and one of the trolls made his usual daily trek to the first car. I didn't know his name; never cared to ask. He claimed he got car sick sitting all the way in the back. His footsteps echoed and rattled the car as he walked by me. I didn't know many of my new schoolmates by name. To me, being in public magic school was only temporary. I was determined to get back into coven school. So that's what I focused on.

Next came the underwater tunnel as the mermaids' subway cars attached to the end of the line. The color of the water outside the windows reminded me of the purplish blue stones of my old school. My mind drifted back to the tallest spire, wondering what potions my friends would try and come up with without me. I bet they were still working on the potion that would make it snow fireworks. I missed Blake, Tim, and Matt. Heck, I even missed Lynne. As I thought about my friends I closed my eyes and must have drifted to sleep.

"Boo!" I yelled, sneaking up on the out of place witches. My friends were hovering outside the front door of the human Halloween party I had told them about obviously debating whether or not to go inside. Lynne squealed in fright and they all turned to look at me. "Ha-ha! Got you," I laughed.

"Chris, is that really you?" Blake asked, not believing his eyes as he looked me up and down. His Harry Potter costume was the same one he had worn last year, but it suited his personality, kind and a bit quirky. "How did you," he started to say as he tugged

29

on my face right below my jaw. My skin stretched away from my bone as though it were Silly Putty then snapped back into place. The black robes I wore moved like they had a mind of their own; trailing behind me and turning into smoke. "You look like you stepped straight out of American Horror Story or something. Man! It feels and looks so real."

"That's because it is," Lynne chimed in. She was dressed like a sexy version of the devil; of course she was. Her costume fit her personality as well, self-righteous, self-absorbed, and forever pissed that I was the only guy in school that wouldn't pay attention to her. "He conjured it. Didn't you, Chris?"

"Chris?" Blake scolded.

"What? Oh, come on!" I got defensive. "Can't we have just a little fun with our powers once in a while? I mean it's Halloween!" I said about to ring the doorbell. "Besides, no one will ever know."

For some reason Lynne gave me an unexpected devious smile and stepped up beside me. "Come on boys, Chris is right. Let's have some fun. Freshen up my costume would ya? I'm thinking Lady Gaga-esque," she said taking my arm and intentionally letting the side of her breast rub up against me.

I flicked my wrist conjuring her a better costume, but also trying to brush her off physically. It didn't work. She was clinging to me like plastic wrap stuck to itself. Under my command Lynne's shoes and barely there red dress morphed into extreme high-end fashions worthy of a music video for Gaga's little monsters. "Anybody else want a re-vamp?" I asked eagerly not wanting to be attached to Lynne for one more second.

"No, you guys go ahead. I think I'm just going to head home." Blake shook his head in disapproval and Tim and Matt stayed behind as well. "Chris, I don't think this is a good idea--,"

"Later, losers," Lynne said cutting Blake off as she opened the door and pulled me inside.

The party was as wild as I thought it would be. With an equal mix of teens and adults. The human teenagers were on their best behaviors, in front of the adults at least, but there was plenty of behind the scenes action going on. Getting my hands on alcohol proved quite easy, especially since my conjured costume made *me look like I was ancient. I'd even thrown in a low ominous voice for good measure. Lynne's conjured glamour I created may have been beautiful and epic, but I had made sure she looked like she was only about fifteen or so. She was finding it extremely difficult to sneak a drink and kept glaring at me every time she failed as though she knew I had done something to impede her party on purpose. Finally looking in a mirror, Lynne gasped, stomped over to me, and threw her non-alcoholic red drink in my face. She stormed off and disappeared into the crowd. I laughed as she finally left me alone, turned the red liquid into a gel, and let it become another layer of my ghastly glamour.*

The hundred year old mansion was full of people dressed up as everyone from Albert Einstein to ZZ Top and everything in between. The night was so fun that as I stepped away from Lynne for the hundredth time, with my drunken judgement I flicked my wrist in a house full of humans without even thinking twice. Time slowed under my will; not enough that any human would notice, but just enough to make the party last a little bit longer. I was getting a lot of female attention and it seemed to be driving Lynne even crazier. Why wouldn't I want that to last forever?

"Buttercream frosting, hmm, what did you just do?" Lynne asked following me into yet another room. I had been trying to ditch her all night and she knew it. As soon as our friends had left she turned into the wicked witch she always did when we were alone. Without my friends as a buffer she was constantly on me, and it was driving me crazy.

"Nothing," I smiled.

Something or someone in the next room drew her attention for a second then she turned her evil glare back to me. "Humph. We'll see about that," she scoffed and quickly stormed off.

"Muahahaha! Guys and ghouls, it's time to announce the costume contest winner!" The DJ said, turning the music down. I barely caught a glimpse of Lynne leaving out the front door and swore I could smell sweet pine as she left. Her costume and facial features reverted back to their un-conjured state as she gave me an evil wave goodbye; almost as if it were a final farewell. But the DJ called my name and I forgot all *about Lynne and my friends' earlier disapproving looks. "Chris Heron, come on down! You wo--,"*

Unexpectedly, all sounds stopped and everyone in the mansion froze right where they stood. No one seemed to be aware of being in a frozen state and unable to move. Drinks being poured didn't spill. The liquids looked like ice dangling in mid-air and people had stopped in awkward positions all around the house. I was in a living three dimensional picture frozen in time and what had me truly terrified was I hadn't done it. I looked around in a panic knowing I wasn't frozen for a specific reason. Someone from one of the covens had caught me using underage magic and I was in serious trouble. I racked my brain trying to figure out who had the power to freeze an entire house full of humans and then it hit me. 'Oh crap!' I thought to myself. Just as I realized who it was, his footsteps echoed off the marble floor and then stopped. A wave of power hit me and I couldn't move; only my eyes remained unfrozen. I was lifted off the ground and pulled toward the grand staircase like a puppet on strings. Abruptly, I came to a stop at the foot of the stairs and was placed back on my feet, but I still couldn't move. The Reagent of all the covens came down the staircase one methodical footstep at a time. Finally at the bottom of the stairs he hovered over me by at least three feet, took in my conjured costume and inebriated state and stared at me stoically for what seemed like an eternity. He never even blinked. 'Double crap!'

"Mr. Heron, come to my office once you're sober, and do bring your parents, hmm?" Then he waved his hand in front of me and everything faded to black.

I was pulled out of my dream by loud laughter as the school subway car came to a sudden stop at our destination. I wiped my mouth. Apparently I had been drooling in my sleep, but I didn't care. Reliving Halloween night in my dream was much, much worse. The same mermaids and elves were giggling about Kris Kringle Jr. visiting school today, confirming that it was in fact happening. Apparently some of their parents worked at Santa's Workshop at the North Pole and had spilled the info. I rolled my eyes. All the girls were going to be fangirling over Santa's son forever now. Fairies, mermaids, elves, even the trolls were going to be gushing about getting to meet the boy that would inherit his father's title one day. *Ugh! Could this day get any worse?*

*

"Chris?" Tinker Bell motioned for me to stay after class as the rest of the students rushed out the doors to jockey for a good spot in the common area to see Kris Kringle Jr.

"Yes, Miss Bell?" *Crap!* I slumped and walked up to the front of the class. This was it! She knew I had planned on skipping school this morning and I was getting kicked out.

"Be a dear and help me make some potions for the mermaids, hmm? I swear, your potions seem to give them human legs hours longer than mine do." Tinker Bell was sending flasks and test tubes floating through the air but stopped buzzing around and looked at me. "What? Don't tell me you're in a hurry to meet Kris Kringle, too?"

"Me? Ah, no," I stuttered, stunned that I wasn't in trouble. Crises averted.

"Good," she said buzzing around the room again. "And you're a good witch too, Chris, even when you have a lapse in judgment." She paused intentionally letting me know without saying the words that she had in fact caught me this morning. My eyes bugged out, as she probably knew they would, but she calmly continued. "I know it's tough, following the rules in the human world, especially with how advanced your powers are. And I hope you can learn to like being here at school away from the covens. It's not all bad, is it?"

"I guess not," I shrugged not knowing what to say.

"Well, come on. Let's get these potions done so you can join the others."

"Ho, ho, hurl," I said sarcastically and I swear I heard Miss Bell giggle.

*

"Hey, watch it!" I yelled, as a group of elf girls late to the meet and greet rushed passed me. They were in a hurry to see Kris Kringle.

"Sorry," one of them apologized. "We only have a little time to spare. Only fourteen more days until Christmas, you know?"

"How could I forget? You guys remind me every ten seconds," I scoffed under my breath. Watching the crowd of girls position themselves to see Santa's son as they giggled and blushed was nauseating. I didn't even know why I was out here. Curiosity I guess.

"I hear he's a real douche bag," a girl's silky voice chuckled beside me.

Surprised to be standing next to the only other person on the planet not excited to meet Santa's son, I turned. But the girl before me was so stunning I was at a loss for words. Long greyish blonde hair, dark blue eyes the color of a glacier's moulin, and skin as pale and luminescent as ice; she was breathtaking.

"What?" She asked, twirling a curl of hair between her fingers. "They said this was the latest color."

I stared at her hair and realized my mouth was open but no words were coming out. "Oh, sorry. No, I mean yes it's nice. It's just I, uh, didn't expect to see a girl at this school who wouldn't be lusting after Kris over there." I said motioning to the horde of girls asking for autographs and taking selfies with him. You had to give magic folks credit though. Who needed a selfie stick when a floating phone would do the job? Actually, there were dozens of phones hovering in the air around Kringle snapping pictures as girls posed all around him.

"Eww, gross. He's like my third cousin twice removed or something like that," she said dismissively.

"Aren't you a little tall for an elf?"

"Shouldn't *you* have green skin and warts on your nose?" She huffed.

"Ha! Touché. Did you just start here?"

"No, I've been here a couple of weeks." She held out her hand and I took it eagerly, "My name's Nichole Frost." Her hand was cold, but I also felt a sort of heat radiate from her skin.

Funny, I would have remembered seeing her before today. She was kind of unforgettable. We ended the handshake, but couldn't help the goofy joke that blurted out of my mouth. "Any relation to Jon Snow? Um, I'm Chris Heron by the way."

"You know nothing, Chris Heron," she teased. "Chris, hmm? Maybe *you're* related to Kris Kringle over there."

"Ha! No way."

"You're probably right," she shrugged her shoulders. "So show me around this place already would ya? Looks like everyone else will be fawning over Kringle the rest of the afternoon."

"I thought you said you've been here a couple of weeks?"

"Pretend it's my first day." She huffed again.

I held the door open for her as we made our escape. "Frost, huh? Any relation to Jack Frost?" I gasped at the prospect and stood in the open doorway, "Is he real?"

Nichole shrugged her shoulders and didn't look back, "Well, winter is coming."

Oh the Weather Outside is Frightful

"So what's it like being the only witch here?" Nichole asked me as we roamed the empty corridors of school.

"Kind of sucks." I tried not to slip on the light snow that was falling around us and turning to water in the hall. No wonder Kringle went to school at the Pole. If weather like this followed him around here, we'd all be shoveling snow just to get to our desks every day or knee deep in water.

"What's it like pretty much being a Kringle but invisible next to golden boy back there?"

"Ha! Golden boy. Now that's funny," her smile was breathtaking. "It's kind of nice actually. I'd hate all the attention he's getting." Her statement was definitive and she seemed dead certain that she would never want that kind of attention, ever.

"Yeah, it'd just be horrible," I said sarcastically. "Who wouldn't want *that* kind of attention?" *Especially from so many girls*, I thought to myself. It was like Kris was a celebrity or something. But, I had to admit, having the attention of just this one girl felt pretty great. I don't think I'd want to switch places with good ole Kris any time soon. "Where'd you go to school before this?"

"The Pole," she stated matter-of-factly.

"The. North. Pole?"

"Yep," she shrugged. "But, after some major negotiations my parents agreed it'd be better if I got a more well-rounded education. How about you?"

"Coven Prep out of New York. Got sent here for using underage magic in the human world."

"Bummer, but, that explains the hat." she paused. "I guess I'm glad it happened."

Confused, I looked at her. How could she be glad that I got kicked out of school? "Why do you say that?"

"We would have never met otherwise."

I felt my face flush. Did she see? How embarrassing. I didn't know what to say. *Don't blow it. Don't blow it!*

"Will you show me around your New York sometime? I've never really gotten to see much of the human world before," she asked shyly.

"Sure. Absolutely," *chill Chris, stay cool.*

"When?" She asked eagerly.

"Whenever you'd like," I shrugged. *Okay, idiot, now you're being too nonchalant!*

"Okay, let's go." She beamed.

"What? Now?" Frantic, I looked around, already feeling guilty for wanting to ditch my afternoon classes.

"Relax. Jeesh teacher's pet much?" Nichole gestured towards the common area where we could hear the crowd chattering and phones clicking as they still hovered around Kringle. "Didn't you hear? We've been dismissed for the rest of the day so we can party with Kringle and I know you're just dying to do that," she mocked. I could almost see the emoticon tongue wag as she said the words.

"Ha! You know me too well already."

"Then let's go!"

*

As we got off the subway and went up the steps the golden light of the magic realm dissolved behind us. I watched Nichole's reaction as we fully emerged into the human world. The sites, smells, and sounds of New York City had her mesmerized. The colors were probably pretty vibrant to her compared to the monotonous reds, greens, and whites of the Pole. Yellow cabs and metallic colored cars whizzed by, human after human walked passed us, and the buildings soared above our heads. Nichole took everything in. She even giggled as a cabbie honked and flipped off another driver.

Nichole inhaled, "What is that smell?"

I sniffed the air. "That's just New York for you. Dumpster trash, car exhaust, and every type of food vendor imaginable from here to New Jersey."

"It smells fantastic! And it's so beautiful here!"
She looked all around, absorbing and memorizing every
new sensation the city had to offer.

"Really?" I scoffed.

"You're lucky to live here, there are so many
wondrous things, it's magical without being magic. All I
ever get to smell is cinnamon spice and pine. And all I
ever see is blinding white snow." Nichole's hair
whipped around her face and brushed her shoulders. I
tried not to get too distracted as I felt another snowflake
touch my face. If snow surrounded this girl I was
beginning to realize I'd suffer an arctic storm just to be
near her.

"Speaking of," I gestured to the sky. It had
started to snow and was really coming down. "Did you
do that?"

She evaded my question with a shrug and a
devious smile. "It's no wonder you're so tempted to use
magic here. I mean it's just begging for it."

"Oh, no. Nichole, don't you dare!" I hissed,
hoping no one was paying attention to us. "I can't!"

"Relax. I know the rules." Nichole began twisting one of her grey blonde ringlets around her finger. With the twirl of her finger the golden shimmer of the magic realm was back, superimposed over the human world. Her gesture when she used magic seemed familiar somehow, but I couldn't place it.

"How did you do that?" I turned in a circle, not believing my eyes. A human walked right through me as he made his way down the sidewalk. "I thought we had to be near a hub, like the subway station, to be able to see both realms?"

She shrugged again. "Inherited it from my dad."

"Nice trick. So now what?"

"Now you show me around New York City *and* we can use magic," she beamed.

So, I was in a bit of a dilemma. On the one hand, I was already on magical probation of sorts. Using magic again outside of school, even with a mystical ice goddess fudging the borders of the realms, could land me in a shit storm of trouble. On the other hand, I was with the most beautiful girl I'd ever seen. And, she wanted to hang out with me. I only had one choice.

"Well who can argue with that? But how do you propose we get around? It's not like we can hail a cab now. They can't even see us." I laughed as people went passed us and through us as they tried to get out of the weather that was getting worse by the minute.

"Have a broom lying around anywhere?" She teased.

"Ha, ha," but I couldn't be mad at her dig, she was too beautiful standing there as shimmering golden snow fell all around her.

"Meh, no matter," she twirled her hair again and in the street materialized a conjured ice blue Lamborghini Aventador convertible. Unknowingly, a human bike messenger road right through it and kept on peddling down the street.

"Hhmm, shouldn't it be red, Ms. North Pole?" I teased her back.

"I like blue better," she shrugged and got behind the wheel. I couldn't disagree there. The color matched her eyes beautifully.

"You know an awful lot about the human world to conjure a car like this."

"We have satellite T.V. and Netflix at the Pole you know? I mean, hello!"

"You have expensive taste," I said climbing in and admiring the super car that I knew had an equally super price tag.

"So my dad keeps telling me." She said dismissively and put her hands on the wheel, "Okay, which way?"

"Oh, you think you're driving?" I chuckled.

"Well I am the one behind the wheel." Nichole raised a perfectly arched brow at me.

"You sure about that?" I waved my hand in the air and the Aventador lifted up off the street and hovered in the air.

Nichole's arms reached out, looking for something to hold onto as gravity became obsolete for the car. As if it were on an invisible road I leveled the car out in the sky and she got her bearings. "Nice trick," she turned and smiled at me.

"Got it from my mom. Broom, car, it's all relative," I chuckled and gave her back one of her signature shoulder shrugs. I was trying to fake an air of chill around me when I realized it was snowing in both realms which seemed peculiar. Instead of searching for a reason why I ignored the snow. I was too focused on the smiles she kept giving me. Smart, beautiful, and wanting to spend time with me over Kringle Jr.? Yeah, I was a goner.

"What is *that* smell though? It's like holiday cookies or," she said looking around for the source.

"Buttercream frosting?" I offered.

"Yeah, that's it," she whipped her head toward me and giggled as she realized that my conjuring magic smelled like dessert. "Oh, Chris, that's got to be miserable for you. I'm so sorry."

I couldn't help but stare into her blue eyes. They had the prettiest gold flecks in them I had ever seen, almost the same color as the magic realm itself. "At the moment, it's actually one of the best things in the world." She turned away, but not before I saw the bluish tint in her cheeks turn a soft pink. "So where to?" I asked trying to lighten the mood.

She turned back towards me and smiled, "Suddenly I'm in the mood for cupcakes with buttercream frosting."

I laughed. "Well you're in luck, I just happen to know a place about ten blocks from here and I bet there's a parking spot right up front with our name written all over it."

"I bet you're right."

"So, it's a date?" I couldn't believe the words just blurted out of my mouth like that. This girl had me unhinged.

"It's a date," she said, surprising me even more.

*

With the flick of my wrist, I lifted the car a little higher into the air and propelled us forward. We watched in awe as our car's reflection jumped from mirrored window to window of the buildings we passed. Humans were working at their desks typing and writing away as if nothing out of the ordinary was going on right outside and ten stories up. Our cruising speed was a comfortable forty miles an hour when all of a sudden another magical car came out of nowhere. It was right in front of us by mere inches. Nichole and I were still just kids and had no idea what the rules of the magic road were. We were going to hit head on. I could see the whites of the other driver's eyes as he tried frantically to steer around us at the last second. We may be magical, but would a car crash kill us? Thousands of thoughts and memories ran through my head before I acted.

"What the--," I read the other driver's lips.

I flicked my wrist and slowed time as I concentrated all my power on avoiding the crash, but it was too late. The cars were still on a slow motion collision course. I sped our car up to normal speed and tried to move it out of the way, but it wasn't fast enough. We were going to hit. Within inches of metal crumpling against metal I protectively reached over and put my arm in front of Nichole. Under my touch, she instantly became aware of our surroundings and the slowing of time all around us. Her survival instinct kicked in and in a flash she reacted. Somehow she yanked our car out of the crash zone so fast that I missed it. We sped off at what seemed like the speed of sound, leaving behind a disoriented driver, and an area still stuck in slow motion. Still protecting Nichole with my arm I looked over my shoulder and flicked my other wrist speeding time back up. As he came to, I saw the other magical driver look around in shock from not having hit us. He wasn't the only one in shock.

"Chris, how did you do that?" Nichole shook her head as she clenched the wheel. "Controlling time, that's a power only the heavy's usually have; your Reagent, the Easter Bunny, the Tooth Fairy, Santa, even I don't--," she slammed the magic car's brakes before we reached the ocean. Palm trees and sandy beaches were the only things below us now, but curiously it was still snowing. We had only been traveling for a few minutes but we were obviously no longer in New York.

"Nichole?" I drew her name out slowly. "Why is it still snowing in what I'm presuming is the southern tip of Florida?" I evaded her question. Looking around I shook my head in disgust. Even the palm trees were decorated with Christmas lights and the lamp posts were adorned with giant stockings made out of tinsel. *Couldn't there be one place not barfing up Christmas? I mean come on!*

She crossed her arms over her chest as the car hovered above the trees. "Well since you saved my life, I guess I'll tell you my secret if you tell me yours." She didn't seem pleased at the prospect of sharing her secret, which to me meant that she really wanted to know my secret. When I didn't say anything she leaned her chair back and put her feet on the dash, "Guess I'll just work on my tan then." With a twist of her hair she conjured a pair of oversized sunglasses and a floppy hat. The snow was hitting her glasses and melting. It was the most adorable thing I'd ever seen. "Good luck getting us back to New York in less than eighteen hours without my help." Then she conjured a timer that replaced the entire front windshield. It began counting down the hours until we were due back at school the next morning.

I wondered how she knew how long it would take to get home without the use of her super speed ability. Time seemed almost instinctual in her. I weighed my options mentally. Even if I slowed time I'd only be able fly the car home at a normal speed. I needed her help and her speed. If I tried to get us home without her help there was nothing keeping her from dropping the veil and exposing my magic to the human world. I was screwed. She had me at a disadvantage and she knew it. If I wasn't back home by morning, not only would I be grounded, I'd definitely be kicked out of another school. And I couldn't let that happen. I was trying to get back into coven school. I had no choice. I had to tell her, but more than that, I wanted to tell her my secret.

"Okay," I sighed.

She popped up and listened intently. "You first," she insisted as her sunglasses, hat, and timer disappeared.

"Ha! I knew you'd make me go first," I chuckled. "Well, my great great grandmother is kind of famous. You may have heard of her," I paused intentionally. The way she was looking at me made my heart beat faster. She was so damn beautiful, I didn't want the moment to end. "And I'd rather not have anyone else know that I'm related to…"

"Yes, yes?" She looked like she wanted to punch me in the arm for making her wait.

"Mother Nature," I whispered.

Nichole gasped. "You're related to Mother frigging Nature? No shi--,"

"Sshh!" I looked around, but we were alone.

"Oh relax, humans can't see or hear us. And there's no one here. Okay, besides the car we almost hit, but that was like so five states ago," she laughed. "Mother Nature really?" she whispered.

I nodded, almost forgetting that she had a secret as well, almost. "And why is it snowing in Florida?"

She sighed, "My name's not Nichole Frost." She looked at me with those mesmerizing glacial eyes of hers, "It's Nichole Claus." And then it hit me. Her mannerism when she used magic; curling her hair around her finger, the way the snow followed her, and the speed she could travel. She even popped up at school claiming to have been there for weeks when I knew she hadn't. As she said the words I knew they were true, "Santa Claus is my dad."

"So does that mean Kringle Junior's your brother?" I asked. The words left a bitter taste in my mouth. She was too exquisite to be related to the walking poster boy for a teen cologne commercial.

Nichole laughed, "Ewe gross, no! There is no Kringle Junior. Well, I guess technically I'm junior. But Barry's great at playing the part, don't you think? He's one of dad's most trusted and loyal elves, and I get a chance at a normal life." She shrugged off all the questions I knew had to be all over my face. "I just want to feel normal. Not hovered over like you saw today because of who I am. No one knows me here. Here, I can be anyone I want."

I lowered the car to the ground and moved it to an un-occupied parking space across from the beach. Nichole lifted the veil of the magic world and the sounds and smells of the human world hit us. A light sprinkling of snow was coming down, but still, it was coming down in a place I knew it wasn't supposed to snow, like ever. I knew we couldn't stay here long. Apparently her growing adolescent powers were accompanied by snowfall like mine had the smell of buttercream frosting.

"I know the feeling." I smiled somberly at her. "So Barry's your smoke screen, or snow screen I guess?" I teased pointing up to the sky.

"Exactly." When she smiled back it took my breath away. "Hey look!" She gestured towards a human bakery with of all things, cupcakes displayed in their window. "Imagine that," she laughed.

"Ha! What are the odds I wonder?" The bakery looked like the most inviting place on earth. It was called Witches Brew and Devilish Delights and was all decked out in Halloween decorations. It even had an animatronic Santa dressed as a witch stirring a large cauldron coffee cup. It was fantastic! I felt my face flush as I remembered I had called this adventure a date, "Shall we?"

Nichole shook her head, "Chris, the snow, I can't."

"Hmm, I have an idea. Put the veil up for a minute." She scrunched her eyebrows together and looked at me curiously. "No underage magic in the human world, remember?"

"Okay, teacher's pet," she teased, but put the veil in place anyway.

I got out of the convertible and went around to the driver side. My heart was beating faster and faster at the prospect of what I was about to do. I took a deep breath and concentrated. Reaching into the sky I flicked my wrist and slowed time just above us within a quarter mile in every direction. I didn't dare go farther out than that for fear of a human seeing a bird hovering in midair or something crazy like that when Nichole dropped the veil. I knew I was pushing the limits of the no-underage-magic-in-the-human-world thing. But, I only cast the spell in the magic world. It wouldn't be my fault if it carried over into the human world. Would it? I know, I know, I was pushing it. Those deep blue eyes had me under their spell. I was willing to do almost anything to make her happy, even use magic where I wasn't supposed to.

As if she read my mind Nichole dropped the veil to the magic world and looked into the sky. Her eyes glistened with happy tears as she looked at the snowflakes hovering, but not falling. I opened her car door and asked again, "Shall we?"

"Most definitely," and she took my hand.

*

"Here we go. Two witches brew white hot chocolates and two devil's food cupcakes with extra buttercream frosting." Nichole and I smiled at each other at the inside joke. "Can I get you anything else?" The owner of the Witches Brew asked us.

"No, ma'am, this is perfect thank you." Nichole said grinning so wide at the normalcy I thought she'd burst into happy tears.

"Please call me Julie, and thank you. I haven't had any customers in here all day. I may just have to shut down early," Julie shrugged her shoulders. "Open back up after the holidays, if I can."

"Why? This place is great." I said. "Anywhere that celebrates Halloween in December is my kind of place."

60

"Aren't you sweet, but around Christmas is my slowest time of year. Guess most folks want everything pumpkin spiced and peppermint frosted," she chuckled. "You kids holler if you need anything."

"We will, thank you," I said as Julie went back behind the counter.

A wall mounted clock in the form of a witch's hat cackled on the hour and the napkin holder on our table was a house. It even had tiny wicked witch legs sticking out from underneath of it decked out in black and white socks and ruby slippers. Decorations that depicted a poor witch being crushed by a house usually made me cringe, but being here with Nichole made them perfect. Julie had even put short bread cookies in the shape of brooms on the saucers of our white hot chocolate.

"I love this place! I've never seen anything like it." Nichole said, as she sipped her drink.

"I guess you haven't, have you?" I stated, realizing just how little of the human world she had gotten to experience. "Even though Christmas is my birthday, Halloween is my favorite time of year," I added, wanting to share new experiences with her, anything to see that beautiful smile of hers.

"Christmas is your birthday?" She quizzed. "No wonder you hate it so much."

"I don't *hate* it hate it." I joked. "I'm beginning to see some good qualities in it," I said looking into her blue eyes.

"I'm beginning to really like Halloween too," she blushed and looked down at her plate.

My attention was drawn to the T.V. which began reporting the weather. The radar was showing a huge cold front coming off the coast right where we were. They were calling it a highly unusual winter storm. Nichole must have seen the shock on my face and turned to the T.V. "We should probably go soon," I said deflated. I didn't want to leave. I wanted this day to last forever.

"You're probably right," she nodded her head and turned back to me. "Thank you, Julie, it was nice meeting you." Nichole seemed sad as she got up from the table.

"Thank you, Nichole, it was lovely meeting you both as well." Julie came to our table with to-go cups and a box for our cupcakes. "It's probably best that you're getting ahead of this crazy storm. I've never seen anything like it. But you two come back anytime, you hear? You are always welcome at Witches Brew."

Nichole looked up and smiled warmly, "Thank you, I'd like that very much."

As we walked out of the Witches Brew and Devilish Delights shop Nichole seemed to deflate. "I'm not going to be able to go to school, not like this," she said pointing to the storm collecting along the coastline. She curled her hair around her finger and returned us to the magic realm. Its golden hue making the sunset a brilliant yellow against the greenish blue ocean. I flicked my wrist and returned the air above us to normal time. The storm dissipated and snow began to fall into both realms again. "I can't hide who I am with snow always falling around me. Barry's visiting the school again tomorrow, but then that's it. He's got to go back to the Pole."

"So yours isn't just when you use magic it's--,"

"It's all the time," she finished my sentence. "Why are you smiling?"

"Because it's a good thing you met a witch today." An idea had hit me and I was grinning ear to ear. "Meet me after school tomorrow. I may just have a remedy for your problem. Or should I say, potion for your problem?"

I'm Dreaming of

"You seem different today, Chris. Happier." Miss Bell stopped flying around her chemistry lab and looked at me. "Did you meet someone?" She smiled.

"Miss Bell." I got embarrassed and didn't answer.

"You're right, you're right. I'm sorry, it's none of my business," she said and examined my new concoction as it cooked. "If it works, this potion will be an amazing feat of magic. It's far more advanced than your years. I mean a potion that can hold Mother Nature at bay? Unbelievable!" Miss Bell was shaking her head in disbelief. "But who's it for? And why would they need such a thing?"

Crap! I couldn't lie to Miss Bell, but I also couldn't reveal Nichole's secret. "A friend of mine's magic tracker follows them into the human world even without them using magic. It's quite disruptive to humans and it has the potential to reveal us all." There, that wasn't a lie and it didn't have to mean that Nichole was Santa's daughter.

"Well, sounds like your friend is very lucky to have you." Miss Bell buzzed around the class room checking the Bunsen burners and the drip tube levels. The potion was slowly filling up a test vial with an ice blue liquid the color of Nichole's eyes. I'd added that touch of color purely for my enjoyment alone. Miss Bell added a new vial below the drip tube and gingerly floated the vial with the test liquid to her desk. She waved her hand and a large glass jar glided off one of her shelves and landed on the table next to the test vial. I poured the liquid into the large jar and stood back. With another wave of her hand Miss Bell activated the liquid and it turned into a benign explosion of snow above our heads before vanishing for good. Miss Bell nodded at me with pride in her eyes, "You better head to your next class before you're late. I'll keep an eye on your potion for you."

"Thanks, Miss Bell. See you after school." I rushed to my next class thinking only of Nichole. I couldn't wait to share the good news with her. She didn't have to go back to the North Pole. She could stay here with me. The potion worked!

*

"I, I don't know what to say." Nichole looked at the blue luminescent liquid as it swirled in the vial.

"Say you'll stay," I smiled. "The potion works here and in the human world."

"Are you kidding? Of course I'll stay!" She took the vial from my hand and wrapped her arms around my neck. "How can I ever thank you for this?"

"Come with me to Witches Brew to celebrate?" I'd done it again. I asked her out without even thinking about it, but I didn't care. I liked spending time with her even if she was the guy in the red suit's daughter. "And to field test it, of course."

She laughed. "Of course." But was she saying 'of course' to the field testing or yes to going out with me? I was confused until she rolled her eyes and held up a learners flying permit with her picture on it.

"How did you get that? And so fast?" I quizzed her.

"I've been flying Rudolf around since I was a kid and well Barry pulled a few strings for me at the DMV."

I chuckled, "Rudolf? Really?"

"Come on!" She grabbed my hand and we headed for the station that would take us to New York City.

*

Nichole had a lot of questions about the potion as we flew her blue convertible at super speed towards Florida's coast. "Are there any side effects? How long does one dose last? How soon will the snow stop after I take it?" She'd admitted to never taking any type of potion before. Which was new to me. Witches and potions were like fairies and pixie dust, you never saw one without the other.

"Relax, Nichole, breathe." I had to laugh a little at her nervousness. It was so cute. As we landed the car in our usual spot I popped the cork on the vial and handed it to her. "Want me to drink one with you?"

She gasped. "What would that do to you?"

"Nothing. It's designed just for you, but if you're scared--," I mocked her.

"Hand it here." Nichole downed it and almost spit it back up as she laughed. "White hot chocolate and buttercream frosting? How did you do that?"

Without even looking up I pointed to the sky. "I'm good with potions."

Nichole gasped again. "Chris, you did it! This is amazing!" Tears filled her eyes as she looked up into a snowless sky. She lowered the veil and the human world enveloped us with no snow in sight. "Oh no!"

I was pulled out of watching her joy, "What! What's wrong?"

"Julie's shop is closed." She pouted. Even her pout unhinged me. We walked closer to the building to read the handwritten sign on the door.

'Dear Loyal Witches Brew Customers, we will be closed until January 1ˢᵗ and hope to see you all after the holidays. Best spells and potions, Wicked Julie.'

"Awe man this sucks! I wish there was some way we could've helped her stay open through her slow time." I took my hat off and pulled my hand through my brown mop of hair.

"Me too. She was so nice," Nichole said and continued after I gave her a confused look. "Julie's the first human I've ever met."

"What? Really?" I was shocked and a bit sad for her.

Nichole nodded her head and looked away. "I've never met a witch before either," she whispered. For some reason that one sentence melted my heart and I had an idea.

"Come on." I put my hat back on, took her hand, and headed back to the car.

"Where are we going?" She asked, but followed my lead.

"A baseball game to have hot dogs and pretzels with screaming fans, the Eifel Tower to take pictures with tourists, and the Colosseum just for its pure magnificence, you name it and we'll go. I'm going to show you the world!"

*

"What is this thing we're going to see called again?" I asked for the tenth time. I couldn't understand why we were headed all the way to Rome, Italy and instead of wanting to see the Colosseum, Nichole insisted on seeing some statue first.

"It's the statue of Pluto and Proserpina by Bernini," she huffed. "And we're here."

"Oh man! You didn't even do a flyby over the Colosseum first?" I slouched in the passenger seat.

"Later. The gallery closes soon. Now will you land this thing already?"

"Okay, okay." I did what she asked. How could I not? She dressed up for her first official outing into the human world in the prettiest long navy blue skirt I'd ever seen. Her grey blonde hair was tied low in a side ponytail and her silver highlights shimmered when she moved. I had to wipe my palms on my pants while we landed. Every time I looked at her they started to sweat profusely. We got out of the car and Nichole lowered the veil. The sun's evening light hit her orange sweater and it created a breathtaking glow about her. It was almost as if her happiness was radiating out of her as light.

Walking into the gallery I got bored pretty fast though. Old oil paintings and statues weren't my idea of fun. But watching Nichole's reaction to them was entertaining. She absorbed the details of every piece we walked passed on our way to *the* statue. Presumably she was admiring the artistry within each work, but I just didn't get the appeal. And then when we walked into a smaller room and saw what we had come for she froze in what I could only describe as awe.

"Wow!" She said breathlessly. "It's even better than I had imagined. I mean, I've seen pictures, but this?"

"It's a guy carrying a girl and they're naked!" I whispered.

She rolled her eyes and walked closer, admiring the detail, "It's amazing."

I scratched my head. "I guess I just don't get it," but I hadn't said it unkindly. I wanted to see it the way she did, I just couldn't.

"A human carved this, by hand," she whispered back. "Bernini didn't wiggle his nose and use magic and he didn't drink a potion to become an artist the easy way. Here look at this," she walked around to the side of the statue where Pluto's hand was gripping Proserpina's upper thigh. His fingers were making indentions in her skin under his grip. Nichole parted the slit in her skirt and demonstrated on her own leg showing the way her skin sunk in under the pressure. "I mean, how did he do that? The way he was able to form the marble like that is simply amazing." For a moment I actually forgot I was supposed to be looking at the statue. Her show of skin had made my palms sweat again and this time my heart was beating fast. Blushing she fixed her skirt and looked back at the statue. I swallowed hard and turned back to the statue and studied it again as well. "Bernini did this one chisel mark at a time into a block of raw marble," her words washed over me as I saw the huge uncut block of marble flash in my mind and the artistry of what Bernini had been able to create out of nothing. "He created beauty out of a solid hunk of rock with his bare hands! There's real magic here, Chris, everywhere. You just have to open your eyes and--,"

"And believe?" I asked and she nodded eagerly. I got as close to Pluto's hand as I could and concentrated on its detail. His small finger was digging into Proserpina's flesh and I swear I could even make out fingerprints on the sides of his fingers. But wait, it was marble, not skin. It was so realistic I forgot I was looking at stone for a minute. "Wow!" My breath caught in my throat. "How *did* he do that?"

She looked at me and smiled, "Now that's real magic."

Santa Claus is Coming to Town

Nichole and I had spent every day together for the past two weeks and even when we weren't flying around in her magic car I felt like I was in the clouds. She was smart, courageous, and beautiful. And I think I was falling for her. Every day after school we'd go on a new adventure around the human world. Yesterday we'd gone to the top of the Empire State Building, she shifted us into the magic realm, and we had eaten a picnic of conjured sweets from some of our favorite places we'd been to. Crepes from Paris, chocolates from Belgium, and of course gelatos from Rome. I didn't just think I was falling for Nichole, I knew I was, and I couldn't wait for today's adventure after school. No matter what it was I knew it would be great as long as I was with her.

Magic folk didn't get a week off from school like most human kids did. In fact, Christmas Eve was the busiest school day of the year for us and we were all required to attend or suffer the consequences. As I headed down to the subway station, snow began to fall in sheets. Crisp white snow was everywhere. It was blinding. I couldn't even see two feet in front of me and wondered if it could have anything to do with Nichole. I shrugged it off as simply winter hitting New York hard right before Christmas. I passed my card over the turnstile and the golden light of the magic realm enveloped me, but something was wrong. A wave of collective sadness hit me, taking my breath away. Then I heard the sobs. Fairies and pixies were crying and I found it odd that there weren't very many elves around. Even the trolls were upset. Everyone's despair clung to the air like a wet blanket I was trapped under. I couldn't get the feeling off of my skin as it tried to seep into my pores.

My coven friends were out of phase, but I rushed towards them, knowing that they'd be able to hear me. "What's going on? Why is everyone so upset?" I asked a somber Blake.

"It's Santa, he's sick," he said. "I heard they can't wake him up. Some sort of sleeping sickness."

"Kringle Junior and most of the elves are down too," Lynne sniffled. "There's whispers that there isn't even going to be a Christmas this year. Hey, where are you going?"

I bolted back through the turnstile, leaving the thick air of despair from the magic realm behind me, and ran smack into a human.

"Hey, watch it!" He grunted.

"Sorry. Sorry," I said.

The force of the impact along with the wind rushing down the steps knocked my hat off my head and blew it back into the subway station. *Dammit!* But I didn't stop. I rushed up the stairs, out of the terminal, and onto the street. I didn't know why I thought Nichole would be in our parking spot, but I had to check. I had to know if she was alright.

*

When I emerged from the subway station Nichole wasn't there. The only thing that greeted me in the human world was a massive snow storm and people rushing to get out of the weather. Deflated and confused about what to do next I pulled my jacket tighter around me and just stood there.

"Yankee Chris! Yankee Chris!" Sam yelled coming up from the subway terminal. His dingy red and green flannel jacket was still a bright contrast to the grey snowstorm and dark jackets most New Yorkers were wearing. I imagined it had been festive and almost jolly and one point in time, but now was caked with dirt and grime from years of living on the streets. "You dropped your hat."

Dumbfound, I couldn't believe my eyes. "Oh wow. Thanks, Sam. I--, I thought it was gone forever," I said, amazed at his kindness to me, a relative stranger, who had judged him moments ago.

"Nah, nothing's ever gone forever. Things that are important always find their way back to us." He handed me my hat and headed back down into the terminal, but turned toward me on the bottom step.

"Merry Christmas, Yankee Chris," Sam said with a jolly wink.

"Merry Christmas, Sam." I had to smile at his positive outlook on life and generous nature. A homeless man with nothing seemed to have everything he needed.

"Chris?" I heard Nichole's sad cry through the storm.

I followed her voice through the snow and wind. She must have sent my name into the human world because I still couldn't see her. Then I saw it. The edges of the magic realm shimmered with its golden light so I stepped through and found her. I ignored the sadness that swept over me again and walked towards the curb. I had to see that she was alright. Nichole was sitting in her convertible as her uncontrollable self-induced snow storm howled around her. Tears were streaming down her face, turning to ice across her cheeks. Her emotions must have made the storm worse. Even my strongest potion wouldn't be a match for an intense emotional spike like this. I flicked my wrist and stopped the snow temporarily from falling right above her and warmed the air. She gave a little sigh of relief. With her emotions this heightened my potion alone wasn't going to have any effect on the weather that plagued her.

Something huge drew my attention and I turned to look at the big blue sack that was strapped to the fin of her Lamborghini. *Christmas presents?* I thought to myself, then looked in the front seat. On the dash next to the passenger seat was a long list of names written in gold lettering. *The Nice List...Holy shi--*

Right then I knew what she was about to do. Even with all the grief in the magic realm assaulting her, she had found the strength to overcome it and carry out her father's tradition, his legacy, and in that moment, I fell in love with her. Without saying a word, I knew what she was asking of me. She couldn't finish the Christmas deliveries alone and it meant we would have to use magic in the human world to do it. It meant *I* would have to use magic in the human world.

Without hesitating a minute longer I jumped in the car next to her and started to examine the Nice List. "Who's first?"

"Chris, I--,"

But I cut her off, "You don't even have to ask me. We're doing this. Together." I looked into her eyes and made a promise, "Your dad and the others are going to be alright." I sent a wish up to my great, great Grandmother Nature and a prayer to the powers that be to make it so. The wind shifted and a sense of peace settled over me. Even Nichole gave a contented sigh as the despair of the magic realm lessened. *Did me having hope in my heart just do that?* I wondered. Nichole was right. Real magic was everywhere. I just had to believe.

Nichole nodded and started to cry again, but this time they seemed like happy tears. "It's not just your abilities that I need, you know?"

Confused I looked at her. Of course it was my abilities, she couldn't do the List all in one night, not without me. "What do you mean?"

"It's you. I wouldn't want to do this with anyone except you," and then she gave me that smile that always stopped my heart. Beneath all the sadness and despair of our realm, Nichole shined through. "I mean, yeah, your abilities help. Maybe just a little bit," she teased.

"Yeah, just a little bit. Come on, Junior, let's do this!" I lifted the car, presents and all, off the city street. Then without a second thought I concentrated all my power and slowed time everywhere, all over the world, and in both realms. *No going back now!* With a flick of my wrist I turned up the volume on the radio and created chiming jingle bells reminiscent of what children heard when Santa's sleigh flew by. I chuckled to myself and brought Nichole up to speed by holding her hand. As soon as she came to she shot us through the air like a rocket.

We were going so fast her words echoed through the wind in slow motion and I had to laugh. "Don't call me Juniorrrrrrrrrr!"

Dashing Through the Snow

Nichole and I had the entire human world to ourselves as we flew through the night sky and it was amazing. We picked a name off the Nice List, maneuvered the car in for a landing, and parked on the roof of a little girl's house in Salisbury, United Kingdom.

As soon as I let go of Nichole's hand she froze. *Crap!* For a moment I forgot I had to remain in contact with her while the rest of the world was in slow motion. *Well this is going to be interesting,* I thought as I touched her hand again and brought her back up to speed.

"Crap!" She said out loud.

"My thoughts exactly. Guess you're stuck with me," I said trying to lighten the severity of this setback.

"Let's get started and I'll try to come up with a solution while you work. I know we can't be attached like this all night if we want any chance of getting through the List." I unstrapped the blue sack of presents and threw it over my shoulder.

Nichole nodded, took a deep breath, and lowered the veil of the magic world, "Ho, ho, ho, and away we go!" She twirled her hair and we were instantly inside the little girl Celine's living room.

With my extra weight in tow we accidently made contact with the family's Christmas tree and knocked it over. Ornaments began falling to the ground in slow motion shattering against the wooden floor like glitter suspended in a clear jell. Then the tree's lights flickered out.

"Yeah, this is so not going to work. We don't have time to fix things all night long!" Nichole hissed. She twirled her hair and righted the tree, conjured new ornaments, and fixed the lights.

I fidgeted one handed with the sack trying to get to Celine's present. "I know, I know. I'm thinking, I'm thinking!" I retorted. She cleaned up the remaining mess we had made and I put the little girl's present under the tree. As soon as the gift left my hands I felt a shift from the magic world resonate all the way into the human world and into me. It felt as though someone had wrapped me in a warm blanket fresh from the dryer. Nichole squeezed my hand and smiled. She had felt it too. Hope and cheer slowly began to re-emerge within our fellow magical beings and it was echoing down to us. They knew somehow someone was saving Christmas and they were celebrating.

Something caught my eye and I smiled. Next to the fireplace was a plate of milk and cookies and a handwritten note from the seven year old Celine that read, 'To Santa, I love you'. It was one of the sweetest things I'd ever seen.

Nichole saw the note and shook her head. I knew she didn't want to disappoint any little boys or girls on this night. The weight of the responsibility of trying to get to everyone on the Nice List was obviously still taking its toll on her. "I need your help, but not like this, you've got your thinking cap on. Please think faster!" Nichole whispered pointing to my lucky New York Yankees baseball cap.

Her comment made a light bulb go off in my head. "You're a genius!" I said pulling her towards the milk and cookies.

"What?"

I handed her a cookie and took one for myself. "Cheers."

"And we are celebrating why exactly?" But she held up her cookie anyway.

"Because you just figured out the solution to our problem. Now take a bite and leave it for Celine to find."

Nichole giggled at the thought of leaving a Santa nibbled cookie for the little girl to find. And apparently she had complete faith that I had indeed figured out a way to get through the entire Nice List. "Well then. Cheers." We tapped our cookies together and each took a bite. She cocked her head because I was still chuckling. "What's so funny?"

"Get ready. You're about to put my thinking cap on, Yankee Nichole," I teased.

*

"So, your hat is going to act like a talisman or something? Keeping me from slowing down like the rest of the world?" Nichole asked once we were back on Celine's rooftop.

"Hopefully, yes. Something like that," I said as we got back in the convertible. "Are you ready?"

"Ready," she blinked at me and I let go of her hand.

I put my baseball cap on her head and tried to concentrate. Even in my grungy blue hat with wisps of her grey blonde hair flowing out she was the most beautiful thing I'd ever seen. I focused all my feelings for her and my magic into a pin point and flicked both my wrists at my hat. Tendrils of golden light flowed out of me and surrounded my hat. Then slowly the light surrounded Nichole in its glow. It were as though my hope and faith had manifested into pure light and created an aura all around her. And then all the light surrounding her went into her.

Nichole took a deep breath in and blinked. "It worked! Chris, you did it," she said pulling me close and hugging me.

We pulled away at the same time and both lingered there for a moment. I desperately wanted to kiss her, but knowing the whole world was waiting I hesitated and the moment was gone.

Nichole giggled. "Watch this," she said twirling a strand of hair between her fingers. In a flash she and the sack of presents were gone.

From Celine's rooftop I looked around the neighborhood and saw a bolt of golden light bounce from one house to the next. I looked on the Nice List as names started to disappear one after the other.

"Cookie?"

"Jeez!" I jumped as Nichole materialized in the driver's seat. "You scared me!"

"Sorry," she said.

"Was that you jumping from house to house?" I asked pointing to several of the homes I'd seen the streak of golden light in front of.

"Yep, pretty cool huh? All thanks to you," she beamed and adjusted my hat on her head. "So, where to next, Mr. Navigator?" And before I could even answer, Nichole twirled her hair and we were off.

*

Nichole smiled at me every time she returned to the car and saw more names had disappeared from the Nice List. The joy and hope resonating from the magic realm had given her a surge of energy and speed the likes I'd never seen before. It was exhilarating to watch her, but I was glad we were almost finished too. If I ate another cookie I was going to burst. I stayed focused on keeping the world in suspended animation while we traveled and tried not to dwell too much on the consequences of me using magic in the human world.

During our gift giving adventure we'd encountered every weather condition imaginable from dry and hot to tropical and humid. Now we were in a place straight out of a holiday snow globe. A blanket of pristine white snow covered the ground and midnight blue skies full of stars twinkled down at us. The air was crisp, cool, and felt alive with magic. I watched in awe as Nichole's light dashed from one house to the next as the last names disappeared off the List. And then the dash of light stopped.

All of a sudden Nichole popped back into the car. "That's the whole List? We did it!" She said and hugged my neck. She was warm and soft, and smelled like sweet peppermint and cookies.

I lifted the car off the last roof and returned the world to normal speed as we flew slowly through the sky. We were silhouetted by the moon as some radio stations started reporting eye witness accounts of seeing Santa flying through the sky in some sort of futuristic looking automobile. Nichole and I laughed as she curled a ringlet of hair around her finger and returned us to the magic realm.

"Wait," she stopped the car suddenly as we made our way back to New York City. "We forgot someone," she said looking at me.

"Who?" I asked scouring the Nice List. "Nichole, we got everyone on the List, there aren't any more names," I said holding it up.

"Julie's not on the List," she looked up at me with hopeful eyes. "The owner of Witches Brew and Devilish Delights?"

"I remember." I looked to the empty bag that had once been full of presents. "But, if she's not on the List the bag won't conjure a gift for her. What do you want to give her?"

"Something from up here," she said pointing to her head. "You may be a potion master, but I've got my mother's legendary cookie recipe and with your help, I'm sure we can put a Halloween spin on it. I want it to be something so delicious and unique to the Witches Brew that it will draw a crowd for Julie all year long. Are you in?"

"Of course I'm in. Let's go."

*

The edge of the horizon was starting to lighten. Midnight blues gave way to pale ice blues and blazing streaks of orange. We'd been flying around for hours trying to organize our plan for Julie's gift, but we were still struggling with it. At one point I even relented and called my parents, barely mentioning the part about underage magic use of course, and they had said how proud they were of me for helping save Christmas. They made me promise to be safe, come home when our quest was finished, and not to have this little midnight adventure become a nightly thing. My parents had been surprisingly understanding and also told me that if I didn't invite Nichole over for dinner soon I would most definitely be grounded. We all had a good laugh and then it had been Nichole's turn to call home. Apparently the out-poor of hope and joy Nichole and I felt resonate into the human world had also woken Santa and the elves from the sickness that had plagued them. No one knew for sure what had caused the sleeping illness, but the elves were already back at work getting things ready for next Christmas and Santa was recovering in his private study. Nichole's mom invited me and my parents to the North Pole for dinner and I had eagerly said yes. From the delicious sounding ingredients Nichole had given me for Julie's new cookie recipe I couldn't wait to taste Mrs. Claus' home cooking. I bet the magical flavors would linger with me forever.

Nichole flew us up near the northern lights and slowed the car. "This is one of my favorite places in the entire world," she said. The colors were magnificent. Swirls of luminous greens shimmered and swirled against the dark blue sky. "Want to see a neat trick?" She asked and I nodded. With a twirl of her hair Nichole reached out and manipulated the changing colors of the Aurora Borealis with her hand. Like treading her fingers through water the colors moved under her command. She made the lime green swirls even larger and brought purple and hot pink streaks to the foreground around the edges. "Isn't it beautiful? I think the different layers of color are just amazing! Pure magic."

Layers, of course! I thought almost jumping out of my seat. "I've got it!" I said, suddenly tearing off the bottom of the blank Nice List. A startled Nichole turned to me, but I held up my finger. I didn't want to miss a single layer of the spell as I interweaved it onto the magical page. Golden tendrils of light swirled around my pen and soaked into the paper, imbuing it with magic. I wrote down an ingenious name above the measurements and ingredients that Nichole had already given me, and was finally able to add the magical touch that would make Julie's shop into a booming success all year round.

Reminiscent of a dessert sandwich, my additions to the layered flavor sensation would each burst into the taster's mouth one by one, while lingering there longer than any human food ever could thanks to my affinity over time. And they would complement everything! Coffee, tea, carbonated drinks…the recipe was perfection! The aroma of buttercream frosting would fill the air and draw people in and the recipe and Julie would have them coming back for more.

"Merry Chriswitches by Witches Brew," Nichole started reading my addition to her family recipe. "Oh my gosh, Chris, these are going to be a huge hit! How can I ever thank you?"

"You just did." I smiled at her. Her thanks was all I needed. My heart filled with joy and pride from being able to help someone in their time of need. Just then the remaining Nice List sparked from the dashboard as a new name began to appear. Golden light began to burn letters onto the blank page. I read the words as they became whole. "Me?" I whispered. I couldn't believe my eyes as I read my name silently again. *'Christopher Aspen Heron.'*

"Of course you." Nichole said undeniably.

"Did you do this?" I asked, holding up the Nice List.

Nichole shook her head. "I wished for it. But, it wasn't me." She was studying the paper as hard as I was when Santa's satchel shifted. My present was now inside, but I didn't need to look. I already knew what it was. There was only thing I wanted for Christmas and she was right in front of me. She had a sad look in her eyes that I couldn't explain though. "Being on the Nice List means something, Chris. It means more than just getting a present. Do you think you'll go back to your old school now? I think this means that you've been given a second chance." Nichole said.

I gave her a mischievous grin before answering, "You know, I think I kind of like being right where I am." I reached into the big blue satchel and grabbed the sprig of mistletoe and held it over our heads, "After all, we only have 364 days before Christmas."

To my surprise and disappointment she curled her hair around her finger and dissolved the sprig right out of my hand. "Well then, we better get started," she smiled and I melted.

"Merry Christmas, Nichole," I said, not being able to help the joy I felt as the words left my mouth.

She giggled to herself at something she thought was funny. "Happy Birthday and Merry Chris, Witch." And then she kissed me.

Epilogue: He's Making a List

"So how's the *sleeping flu* treating you, Nick?" Tinker Bell asked using air quotes as she flew up to the rooftop.

"Oh, you know it comes and goes," Santa said faking a cough.

"Uh huh," Tinker Bell mocked.

"What? I didn't make her deliver to the entire world her first time out. Just a quarter of the Nice List, that's all." Santa beamed at his daughter and her rebellious blue vehicle of choice.

"She did well tonight. You would have been proud."

"Nichole always makes me proud. How's she doing in school? Is her cover still in place?"

"No worries there. No one knows who she is except Chris there."

"Good." Santa gave the young couple a warm smile as he watched them from afar. "He's a surprising young man. They made a great team tonight."

"That they did. Although I still don't know how normal a life Nichole thinks she's going to get at a school full of magical beings."

"Ho, ho, ho! Nichole said she wanted normal, but I know my teenage daughter. She meant a normal life with boys in it. And define normal these days, Tink, honestly." As if reiterating his point, Santa's phone chimed to the tune of Jingle Bell Rock. He pulled it from his pocket and began reading a text. He smiled as he typed a response. "Coming over for dinner tonight? The misses is sending me on a grocery run for her world famous pumpkin quinoa muffins."

Tinker Bell gave him a questioning look, "What, no cookies?"

"Nope. Times are a changing," Santa said rubbing his diminishing belly.

"It's poker night with Pan and the boys. Raincheck on dinner?"

"Always," Santa smiled and let out another thunderous chuckle. "How is the old boy anyway?" He asked drawing his finger down the side of his nose and conjuring a motorcycle.

Tinker Bell shook her head and put her hands on her hips. "Still lost without me just like the lot of you." Santa laughed joyously at her joke as he started the conjured bike. His red suit morphed into dark red leathers, more suitable for riding.

Santa pulled the Naughty List from his pocket and looked at the name being magically written in the blackest of inks. *Lynne Monty. Well what do you know?* He chuckled to himself and looked back at the young couple. "What's going to happen to Chris now that he broke the rules and used underage magic in the human world again?" Santa quizzed.

"He used magic?" Tink grabbed her chest in mock surprise and giggled. "This is the most magical night of the year you know? So I can honestly say I didn't see anything out of the ordinary."

"Ho, ho, ho, Merry Christmas, Tink," With a wink and an intentional touch to his nose Santa left the couple to their discovery of Chris's name on the Nice List and the anticipation of a first kiss. He flew off the rooftop and into the sky.

Tinker Bell smiled up at him as he flew away, "Merry Christmas, Santa."

About the Author

Have you ever watched a cat stare up at a wall, tracking something's movements-- something invisible that sent shivers down your spine? Did it seem as if your pet were able to sense dark shadows lurking where the veil between worlds and reality thins? That's precisely where the idea for the Netherwalker Series came from for CK Dawn.

Award winning author, coffee loving gamer girl, and Sci-fi enthusiast, CK Dawn has always loved to snuggle up with her cat Hagrid (the shadow-seer) and read. With a nudge of encouragement from her lil' sis, she found writing fantasy stories was even better than just reading about them. So, a long time ago in a galaxy far, far away CK let her unique tale of knights and Camelot dancing in her mind take form and fly with Cloak of Shadows, her award winning debut novel. In writing, CK has truly found her bliss and now writes her enticing, mystical fantasies in the witching hours with Hagrid by her side. Stay tuned, because there will be a lot more to come in the Netherwalker Series. Seriously, the story has only just begun.

CK loves connecting with readers and hopes to hear from you soon.

Website www.ckdawn.com
Facebook www.facebook.com/ck.dawn.cloakofshadows
Twitter @CloakedCKDawn
Instagram @ck_dawn

Please enjoy this sneak peek of

**Cloak of Echoes from the Netherwalker
Series!**

CLOAK OF ECHOES

A Netherwalker Short Story

CK DAWN

Just as Emma Kincaid came into some disturbing empathic powers, she lost her mother in a car crash. She is also pretty certain she's being followed, maybe even hunted. But, is it the shadowy creatures that haunt her nightmares or the mysterious guy, shrouded in darkness, who just enrolled at Jefferson High?

**Monsters haunt her dreams, but humans are her worst
nightmare…**

PROLOGUE: LETTER WRITING

Rachel Kincaid looked up from the letter she was writing and stared at her baby girl sleeping soundly in her crib. *Stay small as long as you can little one. The shadows may be real, but we still have time.* Rachel felt a tinge of guilt patter out of her heart and into her throat. Emma was an absolute blessing, but her arrival had changed everything. Rachel was used to keeping secrets from others, even from her loving husband, but now those secrets wouldn't be hers alone to keep. They would be passed on to her innocent daughter. All Rachel wanted was a normal docile life for her daughter for as long as she could give it to her, but plans had to be put in place. She looked at the letter in her hands and shook her head.

Just then the wind kicked up and whistled through the nursery's open window. The young mother got up and rushed to the window to close it. Lightning struck the ground in the distance and illuminated the entire sky for only a fraction of a second, but it had been enough.

Rachel's attention and head snapped to the end of the alley as the thunder cracked in the darkness. Out of the corner of her eye she saw it. An out of place shadow shifted and slithered away rattling and vibrating with power. *You can't have her,* she thought. *You will never have her!*

Rachel's emotions must have stirred Emma. Even while sleeping the newborn sent out soothing thoughts to her that filled Rachel with an empathetic warmth that she dreaded. The comforting sensation had been instinctual in her daughter from the moment she was born and was the cause for Rachel's concern. She went to the crib and touched Emma's cheek reassuring the sleeping babe that everything was okay.

The thunder must have woken her husband. Rachel could hear his footsteps just outside the nursery door. Robert peered in and whispered, "You girls okay?"

"We're fine," Rachel whispered back.

"Coming back to bed?" he smiled.

"In a couple more minutes."

Robert yawned. He'd been working double shifts in preparation for Rachel's maternity leave. "Let me know if you need anything, my love."

"I will, my love."

Robert shut the door and Rachel heard him walk back down the hallway to their bedroom. *Should I tell him?* It was the question Rachel struggled with even before they had married. Sighing, she picked her letter back up, sat in the overstuffed nursing chair, and began writing again. She couldn't help the tears that fell as she signed it and placed it in a manila envelope. Pulling out her phone she glanced at Emma again before sending out a long overdue text. '*It's done.*'

SANITY FADING

Emma Kincaid tried to scream but no sound escaped her throat. She gasped for air in the barren desert surrounding her but the atmosphere was too thick to breathe. Her brown hair floated all around her, framing her face like a halo. Then she remembered she didn't have to breathe here. The air's gelatinous texture was heavy enough to write in. Mesmerized, she traced scrolling patterns into it with her fingers then erased them and traced more designs into the translucent air. But something in the back of her mind was warning her to keep moving. With hands outstretched in front of her, Emma pushed through the atmosphere blindly. Everything was alien to her here, even the orange dirt that ground between her teeth seemed foreign and bitter.

She searched the gel trying to find a way out as invisible hands tightened a grip around her neck. Emma's flesh was being peeled away from her bones strip by strip.

Pieces of her skin weren't being ripped off quickly like a Band-Aid; something was methodically removing and savoring each morsel. A monstrous, contented cackle echoed off the jagged cliffs high above. Emma followed the sound and was instantly transported to a cave within the tallest peak. Teetering on the cliff's ledge she watched the creature that had become all too familiar to her now. It sat on a throne made of bones and skulls plucking things from the air and consuming them. It wore black armor that clung to its emaciated bones like a liquid skin. The flowing edges of material that touched the ground were frayed. Ravenous beasts cowered at its feet clawing at its armor for attention. The creature looked at Emma and plucked another morsel from the air. With each bite the creature took, Emma weakened. As the horror of being devoured sank in Emma threw herself off the precipice and bolted upright in bed.

Emma sucked in a breath as she tried to slow her heart rate. As the nightmare faded she quieted the alarm that had apparently been going off for the last five minutes. She got out of bed and rushed to her window shutting out the chill that had enveloped her room. Emma swore she could see her breath as she struggled with the latch. Her dad must have opened it during the night. Emma never left it open anymore. Her nightmares had made her paranoid. So even though their New York apartment was ten stories up she kept her window locked tight. Thinking of her dad, Emma concentrated on her surroundings. *Good, dad's still asleep*, she thought rushing to get dressed.

With breakfast made and her dad waking up, Emma grabbed her backpack and yelled at her father's closed bedroom door. "Bye, dad."

His bedroom door creaked open and the disheveled man poked his head out. "Try and have a good day at school today okay, honey?" Robert Kincaid said and looked at his daughter with the sympathetic expression he always seemed to give her now.

"I will. I love you, dad." Emma said, planting an artificial smile on her face for him before heading to their front door. She often wished she could have a genuine smile. Emma couldn't remember the last time she really smiled or felt happy.

"I love you too, honey." Emma's heart threatened to burst as he matched her forced smile. She was sure she would have been convinced he was letting go of his worry over her if it weren't for her recent 'emotional radar.'

As soon as Emma closed the front door to their apartment her earbuds went in and her hood went up, creating a cocoon of solitude against the bombardment of people's feelings all around her. Her father's emotions were the worst. Ever since her mother had died in the car crash, Robert Kincaid's emotions had almost overwhelmed Emma. He didn't have to do or say anything, Emma simply felt his pain and grief, almost as if she were an empath. Over time, the intensity of his emotions lessened as he made his way through the grieving process. Unfortunately, other people's feelings started to seep in and her dad still had a lot of grieving left to do. Soon after, Emma could feel everyone around her. She thought maybe she was going crazy with grief herself, but it had been over two months since her mom passed away and the sensations were not dissipating. They had only grown stronger. Emma had just learned to turn the volume down as it were by distracting herself with other things. She cranked up the volume on her music and prepared herself for a long dreary day of high school.

Emma cut through the alley that her father specifically told her to avoid, but she couldn't help herself. It took fifteen minutes off her walk to school and kept a lot of the random passing cars' occupants out of her head. The anger coming off some New York drivers scared her more than any dark alley ever could. Pressing her earbuds further into her ears, she cloaked herself from all the echoes of emotions that radiated down to her from the towering buildings above and went deeper into the belly of the short cut. The dark shadows of the alley cast a gloomy grey hue onto the slick pavement reminiscent of how Emma felt. Shiny on the surface, but dark, dreary, and damaged in the crevices where most people never cared to look. She desperately missed her mother, the one person she thought she could talk to about what was happening to her, but Emma was alone. Her father seemed to be okay on the outside, too, but experiencing his feelings first hand day in and day out, Emma knew that he felt lost and helpless without the love of his wife, Rachel. Some days it seemed the only thing that kept him going was his commitment to Emma. That was a heavy burden for a seventeen year old to be privy to, or anyone for that matter. Knowing that her father was willing to give up on life if she wasn't around was brutal. So every day she shut down her own emotions and put on a smile for her dad and every day he became a little more like himself.

Two weeks ago a lawyer had given Emma an envelope stating it was from her mother with instructions to be opened on her seventeenth birthday. The letter still sat unopened on her dresser. Her birthday had come and gone with little reason for celebration. Emma worried that reading it would shatter what little sanity she had been able to scrape together. Her mom would truly be gone and she would break. So the letter sat on her dresser collecting dust and she stayed strong and unfeeling for her father.

Emma jumped at a noise. She scanned the area, convincing herself the loud crash was probably caused by a feral cat rummaging for food. Her determination to stay away from as many people as she could far outweighed her fear of the creepy alley, but still, the alley was creepy. Dark clouds swooped in, hiding the sun. The fall winds picked up, rattling a few tin cans further down in the darkest parts of the alley. Emma looked up into the sky, wondering if it was about to rain when she was hit by a wave of euphoria followed by a calm she hadn't felt since being sucked into everyone else's emotions. Everything and everyone turned to silence and she was alone in her head for the first time in what seemed like forever.

Emma cried joyous tears as peace washed over her. She removed the earbuds she had jammed into her ears and tried to steady herself in the tranquility she was experiencing. Something nagged at her. Muffled instincts were telling her something was wrong. The sensations were too close to what she experienced in her nightmares. As she brushed away her tears, her palms began to sweat and her heart raced. Emma tried to focus on what could possibly be causing both the calmness she was feeling and her incongruent anxiety. The silent void felt forced, foreign, and intrusive as it expanded to include a sensation of unexplained happiness and warmth. An underlying element of being something's prey had Emma truly scared. Pushing past the euphoria, Emma stepped out of the shadows and into a sliver of sunlight peeking through the clouds. Fighting for control, her flesh began to feel like it was being torn from her bones, strip by strip, as her life force was ripped from her body droplet by droplet. The sensation felt almost as though she were being consumed, just like in her nightmares.

Emma gasped as frigid air filled her lungs, burning on its way down. The sun disappeared. As she exhaled, her breath was visible all around her. The chill in the air should have been unbearable, but something in her mind was telling her she was happy and safe. Taking in a deep breath, Emma tried to cleanse herself of the feeling that someone or something was marking her with a brand. It was claiming her, beginning with her scorched lungs. Whatever was causing the sensation, she was determined to find its source for she was certain she was in mortal danger.

Looking frantically around, wondering where this threat could be, Emma rummaged through her pockets trying to find her pepper spray. She knew it might not do any good, but she was desperate for any advantage. Slowing her breathing, Emma carefully put her back to the nearest wall and scanned the alley once more. Nothing seemed out of place. Shaking her head trying to dislodge the cloud that had begun to shroud her mind, she attempted to focus on what was real and tangible. Her heart began to pound audibly in her chest as she realized that the sensations weren't coming from a person or anything even remotely human. *The creature from the cliff!* She had no idea how the nightmarish creature was able to surround her with the feeling of pure bliss but she ran away from it and the cold as fast as she could. She would have enjoyed staying in the silence if she wasn't so frightened of the creature from her nightmares and its power. Just as that thought crossed her mind, a low angry rattle deep in the darkest crevice of the alley behind her began to shake. In spite of her instinct to keep running, Emma turned and finally saw the source of the strange encounter. She watched as an out of place shadow shifted and moved deeper into the darkness. Emma stood frozen for a few moments, trying to make sense of the scene she had just watched. Her hands found the earbuds dangling at her side and absent mindedly placed them in their proper spot as her feet moved once more towards school.

Emma's heart had finally stopped racing and the strange fuzziness in her mind started to dissipate as she reached the front doors of Jefferson High School. She tried to convince herself the encounter had been a figment of her imagination, residual fright from the hellish nightmares that plagued her every night. Emma kept her head down and her music up as she walked through the hallway to class. She knew all her schoolmates intimately without ever talking to them. Patrick, a football player was anxious, sweating, and his heart was beating faster than normal as he contemplated taking the steroids another player had offered him. Janet was grumpier than usual as she awaited her period that was due in about four days, or at least, she was hoping she would get it. Three teachers in the lounge were smoking near an open window, one even had a nicotine patch on his arm, and Emma's geometry teacher was drinking alcohol in his morning coffee. How did she know all of this? Everyone's dopamine, endorphin, and adrenaline levels tickled her skin like they were actual tangible textures. Dopamine felt like soft silky cat fur sliding through her fingers. Endorphins were the wind-pressure on her skin driving with the window down, creating waves with her hand at sixty-five miles an hour. Adrenaline was like being in the front seat of a roller coaster right before the first steep fall. She knew it from the lurch in the pit of her stomach. Emma wasn't exactly certain she could sense the actual neurochemicals firing in the brains of everyone around her, but making it a sort of name-game helped her deal with the intensity of it all. She had learned to enjoy the sensations that came from being a freak, but being hit by all of them all at the same time all day long became overwhelming. Trying to not to look like a freak while managing all of them was nearly impossible.

Emma pulled her hood down but kept her music on until Mrs. Blake actually started her class. As soon as Mrs. Blake gave Emma her usual disapproving look Emma took her earbuds out and prepared as best she could for the onslaught of emotions that she would have to bare for the rest of the day. As the daily assault of teenage angst began Emma tried to pay attention to Mrs. Blake's lecture. She was mostly managing normalcy until there was an unusual void outside in the hallway that shouldn't have been there. Immediately, her attention was drawn to this inexplicable *absence*. She could sense that something or someone was right outside the door, but couldn't feel anything from them. Emma's heart began to race for the second time today, thinking about the thing from the alley. Had it followed her to school? And then the anomaly stepped into the classroom.

Mrs. Blake was saying something about him being a transfer from a private school, but all Emma could do was stare. He was painfully beautiful. She imagined this is how models for Grecian Gods would have looked. Emma was mesmerized by the six foot tall, shaggy, chocolate-haired specimen. Even under his leather coat and dark shirt,

Emma thought she could still make out the contours of his toned muscles.

Gorgeous and unattainable! Emma scoffed to herself, *and probably some type of werewolf or bloodsucker with her luck.* Being of average height with hazel eyes so dark they might as well be brown and mousy brown hair she never knew what to do with, Emma had always felt invisible, especially to boys. Even without her freakish empathic abilities she knew she was a bit odd, or quirky as her only friend Mel liked to say. She had never felt like she really fit in with other teenagers, either, and no one in school ever paid any attention to her. So why should this beautiful specimen be any different? And then, it happened. As Mrs. Blake said the boy's name he looked directly at Emma and smiled.

"Class, this is Mattox Daniels."

Mattox's blue eyes locked with hers. His smile seemed so genuine that she couldn't believe it. Emma's heart got stuck in her throat as she tried to swallow. She tried to smile back but failed. The moment passed and he looked away. Then Mattox took a seat all the way in the back of the classroom far from her own.

I was in his line of sight, that's all, she convinced herself. Besides the void in space he created there was something odd about the boy. Emma couldn't explain it, but somehow she knew he was different from the thing in the alley. She hadn't felt any emotions from him and yet she felt connected to him. *Is he even really here?* She looked behind her and Mattox smiled at her again, still not giving off any emotions. Emma's heartbeat quickened and his smile grew wider with every beat of her heart. She quickly turned back around, but not before Patrick the steroid-contemplating jock chuckled from beside her.

"Keep dreaming, Emma Dilemma," Patrick scoffed. "You'd have a better chance with me, freak," his football buddies laughed along with him.

Emma didn't respond. Instead she stoically looked straight ahead and tried to become invisible. *Well, Mattox is definitely real alright.*

Emma walked down the hall to her next class fully aware of the void in space that followed behind her. She gave a quick glance over her shoulder and could have sworn that Mattox turned away just before she made eye

124

contact with him. She took a detour and made a sharp left turn ducking into the girl's bathroom.

What the hell is going on? She shook her head thinking that maybe the encounter in the alley had done something to short circuit her already crazy wiring. *He can't just NOT be there.* Emma found herself both irritated and intrigued by Mattox. She was curious about her reaction to him, how she couldn't actually get an empathic feel from him. The only thing more powerful than her curiosity, however, was her self-doubt in the face of his ridiculous good looks. Emma couldn't help but instinctively push out her senses to fix on his location. She was certain she felt him pass the bathroom doors and enter her next class. *Oh, you've got to be kidding me!* Two girls came out of a stall whispering and looking at Emma as they left the bathroom in a cloud of giggles. They were probably wondering why she was just standing against the tile wall like a freak staring into space instead of at least looking in the mirror, or gossiping about Janet's period as they had been. Emma walked to the sink and threw some cold water on her face preparing for another hour with the curiosity that was Mattox Daniels. So focused on Mr. Mystery, Emma hadn't noticed this particular distraction had been drowning out a lot of the other constant and intrusive emotions swirling within her perception.

"Mr. Daniels, I don't know how S.B. Devere Academy is run, but here at Jefferson High students are actually expected to participate in class." Mr. Grey mumbled something about private schools and paltry public funds under his breath before turning back to his cracked and faded chalkboard.

Mattox put away the very expensive looking device that Emma didn't think was a phone or an iPad and gave Mr. Grey a halfhearted apologetic shrug.

"My man, Ox," one of the jocks whispered obviously impressed by the gadget.

"You mean fox," a varsity cheerleader chimed in probably hoping for a ride in the equally expensive car Emma assumed he had. Or the cheerleader was simply looking to ride him.

Some of the other students turned to look at him with reverence. And with that, Mattox's fate was sealed. He was officially dubbed a cool.

†

Emma's other morning classes had been uneventful and unoccupied by the curious Mr. Mattox Daniels. She was somewhat relieved, but his absence served to pique her interest even more.

Emma looked at her tray of food made up of entirely beige contents and took a seat. Lunchtime was unbearable. So many people, so many emotions. Emma sat at the farthest bench in the outside courtyard that she could find, but it still wasn't far enough from all the tumultuous teen static.

"Hi. Mind if I sit here?" A voice asked Emma as she hid underneath her hood. Without even looking up she knew it was Mattox that had asked the question and he still wasn't giving off any emotions.

"Sorry, it's taken." said Emma, fidgeting with the fork on her tray. She wasn't quite sure why she wasn't up for his company, but she knew she was still trying to get a handle of the new tumult of her own emotions. Even a small conversation with him might cause her to explode. Emma looked up in time to see his smile replaced by a deflated look of rejection as he looked at her empty table.

"Oh, um. Well, maybe next time then." Mattox seemed to deflate a little as he walked off to find another empty picnic table. His table only remained empty momentarily as a swarm of students descended. He was immediately surrounded as the cool click tried to induct him into their group. Emma watched as they called him names like Ox and Mad Max, slapping him on the back as they sat down to join him. Emma snickered sarcastically to herself. *Well, they could always use another handsome brooding guy to join their ranks.* Mattox didn't join in their banter though. He looked straight at Emma and gave her a mischievous smile that said 'game on.'

Her view of Mattox was abruptly blocked by a mess of bushy blonde hair and thick, wide rimmed glasses. "Who was that?" her friend Mel asked sitting down across from her.

"New guy."

"New hotness you mean. Didn't I see him at our table?" Mel asked, taking a huge bite of her chicken salad sandwich.

"Just lost, I guess." Emma said, pushing the tan food around her tray. "Or maybe he thinks my name is Charity Case, not Emma."

"Ha ha, you're so beyond help, hasn't anybody told him that yet?" Mel said sarcastically as she glanced at Mattox again.

Emma rolled her eyes but had to giggle.

"Well, kidnap him next time would ya? I mean, seriously, Me-ow!" Mel giggled back.

Mel was easy for Emma to be around and not get bombarded with emotions. She, too, had lost a parent and kept her emotions locked up tight, choosing to be fun and carefree instead. Mel's father had died of a heart attack last year and she and her mom had moved from Dallas to New York right after his funeral.

The rest of Emma's day went as usual and there were no more Mattox sightings, but it seemed that she would be sharing her first two classes with him for the remainder of the year. She almost forgot about lunchtime, too, and had to giggle to herself that someone like Mattox had even approached her. She felt a little guilty for telling him her entire table was taken when in reality it was only ever her and Mel that sat there.

Ten minutes left before school let out and she could finally return to her cocoon of solitude. Emma looked out the window and saw the remnants of the sun fading behind a thick blanket of grey clouds. *Rain? Just great.* Considering she had left her money at home, a cab ride was out and the short cut through the alley was definitely out. Emma rolled her eyes at the prospect of a cold rain drenched walk home. *Perfect.*

Rain Numbing

Her chattering teeth almost overpowered the music blaring in her ears. Emma was soaked and freezing, but she was also smiling from ear to ear. She found the downpour exhilarating. Somehow the heavy rain was acting like a shield against all the emotions that plagued her daily life. She would take a nice hot shower instead of her normal bath when she got home to see if she could replicate the glorious effect.

All of a sudden a cab pulled up to the curb and its back window rolled down. Emma pulled her earbuds out and was ecstatic to learn the rain's effect was still intact even without the aid of her music.

"If you want, I know a seat that's not taken." Mattox smiled at his own joke and gestured to the empty seat beside him.

In that moment, Emma felt so normal. Suddenly finding herself without a care in the world, she decided to play along and run a little experiment in the process. "It's just a light drizzle," she laughed, enjoying the liquid curtain that surrounded her. "I'm sure it will clear up any minute now." The rain was coming down in sheets and even Mattox was getting pretty wet from inside the cab.

"Come on, Emma. I'll even have the cab drop me off first so you don't think I'm stalking you to find out where you live." He opened the door and scooted to the far side.

How does he know my name? She hadn't even thought about him stalking her for real. Was he? No, now she was just being silly, still giddy from the break in the emotional assault she was always under.

"Get in here already, would you? My treat."

That sealed the deal for Emma. Also, she didn't want to get hypothermia, so she dove into the cab. The rain's shielding effect was holding even from inside the cab, as if it were a bubble of steel and glass protecting her from the outside world. *Hmm, well that's interesting*, she thought as the driver's emotions surfaced. Apparently since the cabbie was shielded from the rain along with her, her empathic abilities still worked on him. He was mentally preoccupied with a medical exam he was studying for. Emma wondered if walking down the street in the rain under an umbrella with someone would have the same effect as a vehicle. Her heart did a little skip as she thought about who she would want with her under that umbrella as she looked at Mattox. Being so isolated enabled Emma to focus completely on Mattox and his ever present lack of emotionally occupied space. "So where to?" She beamed, concentrating on his facial expressions, tone, and responses. It was refreshing to feel normal again.

"Seriously? I was kidding about dropping me off first. In this rain it'd be about a thirty minute cab ride one-way."

"Seriously?" She thought about it for a minute, "Okay."

Mattox looked into her eyes as if he were trying to figure her out. "Well, okay then," he smiled and turned to the cabby, "Madison Avenue and East Seventy-Fifth Street please."

"You got it." The driver was happy for the long fare and the time to study mentally.

Emma's eyes got big. "Do you live in a castle or something?"

"Or something," Mattox shrugged.

"What on earth are you doing at Jefferson?" she asked trying to get any emotion from him.

"Would you believe I'm on a secret mission?" he teased.

"You'd be surprised what I believe, but from you? No, I don't believe it."

Mattox laughed. "Fair enough."

Emma looked out the cab window not knowing what to say. She hadn't realized how heavily she relied on knowing someone's emotions until now. Her torture device had become her crutch.

"Do you need to call your dad, let him know what you're doing?" Mattox reached in his pocket and held out his phone.

Emma tried to hide the fact that his question sent a chill down her spine. She thought perhaps it was a lucky guess that he suggested her dad and not, say, her mom or her parents. Emma decided to play coy. She would be on guard, but she just had to find out what the deal was with this guy.

"And, what am I doing?" she teased.

"Stalking me?" he teased back.

"Ha, you wish."

"Maybe," he smiled and put his phone away. "So tell me something about yourself."

"No. You first," she stated, not meaning to sound so defensive.

"Well, I started at a new school today, I found lunchtime quite amusing since my attempt to make a new friend was thwarted, apparently by a lunch table occupied by dozens of invisible people," he chuckled.

Emma rolled her eyes and changed the subject, still embarrassed by how she had treated Mattox at lunch. "No, I mean tell me something I don't know."

"Okay," he thought about it for a minute. "I have a younger brother named Malcolm and a cat named Amelia."

"Ooh, so mysterious," she still wasn't getting any emotions from him. "I wouldn't peg you for a cat man."

"Amelia is my brother's really," he smiled at her again. "Mystery, huh? Isn't that what most typical girls want?"

"I'm not typical," she didn't know what else to say, but she was also trying to get him to expose his emotions somehow.

"I know you're not," he looked out the window for a while like he was contemplating something. "I think it's your turn. Tell me something I don't already know about you?"

Emma was taken aback by his comment and decided to try and shock him into exposing some emotion. "I have an unopened letter from my dead mother."

"Oh?" He didn't seem surprised. "What are you waiting for?" His tone wasn't unkind, but still she couldn't get a read on his emotions.

Emma shrugged not wanting to explain the reason. She looked out the window for a long time while the buildings got taller and more expensive. Everyone's emotions were still dulled by the rain and she started to feel an unusual tug towards the area of Manhattan they were headed. It wasn't uncomfortable, but it was definitely a pulling sensation, almost like a yearning. Emma wondered if it had always been there, hidden just below the surface by the other feelings that always overwhelmed her.

"I'm sorry about your mom," Mattox finally said, seeming to watch her reaction to their surroundings.

In the distance a beautiful building came into view directly across from Central Park. "You live in the Vaughn?"

"You've heard of it?"

She nodded, not remembering exactly how she knew the building's name or what it looked like, "Pretty fancy."

"It's home."

"It's a palace!"

"Would you like to see it?"

His question gave her pause. Emma struggled with conflicting emotions. She was leery of this mystery guy but so terribly intrigued by him at the same time. Her stranger danger seemed to be on the fritz in the presence of Mattox. *Could he be working with the shadow creature* somehow? She thought. Emma visibly shivered this time, but tried to turn it into a convincing head shake.

"Maybe next time."

"Well, the invitation is open, anytime," he smiled.

"Thanks," she scrunched her eyebrows together. "How young is your brother? Why doesn't he go to Jefferson?"

"Ah, now there's your mystery," he laughed. Mattox instructed the driver to take Emma wherever she wanted to go, tipped enough for three rides home, and got out of the cab. "Thank you, oh gallant knight, for the safe escort to my humble castle." Mattox teased her through the open window.

"Ha ha, you think you're clever," Emma prodded.

"Oh, if you only knew." Mattox bowed at the waist, "Until the morrow at school, Lady Emma."

She laughed. "So which is it? Am I a lady or a knight?" she asked sarcastically.

"Who says you can't be both?" he smiled.

"Um, every book I've ever read and every movie I've ever seen?" she replied.

"Humph. Funny, you don't seem like the type."

"The type of what?" she asked.

"The type of girl that would let anyone define her." Mattox looked down at her and smiled. "Don't let anyone tell you who you can or can't be." He was so sincere it almost frightened her. "Goodnight, Emma the Fair *and* Brave," and with that he tapped the roof of the cab and the driver drove away.

The tugging feeling was still there, almost as though it wanted her to go back to the Vaughn, but now Emma wasn't sure where exactly it was coming from. Was it coming from the building itself, or was the pull coming from the boy that was still standing on the curb watching her leave?...

Mattox must have been running late to lunch. Out of curiosity Emma turned towards the school and searched for his presence. She tried to convince herself that it was merely an experiment and had nothing to do with her attraction to him. She searched the farthest corners of the school to no avail.

"Let me guess, it's taken?" Emma jumped at the laughing voice behind made. Mattox was outside the school grounds leaning on the metal bars surrounding Jefferson High.

"If you know the answer why do you keep asking?" she said, trying to slow her heart rate.

"Glutton for punishment, I guess," Mattox gave her a sly smile.

"What are you doing out there?" Emma asked.

"Sorry, that's need to know."

"And I don't?" she quipped.

"See, you're not just a pretty face," he smiled sincerely.

Emma blushed. *Does he really think I'm pretty?*

"Have you read your mother's letter yet?"

For a moment his question caught Emma off guard. Her posture stiffened as she responded, "Sorry, that's need to know."

"That's a no," he stated, but his tone wasn't unkind. "So, same time next week then? I'll ask if your entire table is taken, you'll say yes..." he teased.

Emma couldn't help the giggle that erupted out of her belly and for that brief moment everyone's emotions around her ceased to exist almost naturally.

"Ah, there she is," Mattox stated.

"Wha- what do you mean?" Emma asked.

"Nice to finally meet *you*, Emma Kincaid." He gave her another sly smile before walking down the street. "Talk to you Monday!"

Emma shouted after him, "Why are you so interested in that letter?" He didn't turn around or give any indication he had heard. She figured he was too far away to hear, but still had to ask the question. Some of the students around Emma stared at her, she felt their dismay, but she didn't care. *Who is this guy?...*

Emma stayed in her room most of the weekend, telling her dad she had a ton of homework. It wasn't true, but she needed the time alone to recover from the hours at school and the never ending emotions that followed her. Besides the nightmares, playing a game of mental dodgeball against hundreds of students was taking a toll on her and she was losing the game. Emma laid in bed with the covers over her head and tried to drown out her father and the neighbors' senses. After the reprieve the downpour had given her the other day, Emma was disappointed to find out her shower hadn't been able to create the same effect. But it was supposed to rain again today, so Emma waited. Maybe the answer was the creation of so much ozone. Whatever it was, it had been glorious and Emma was desperate for more.

Relief finally came as Emma heard thick raindrops start to fall and clatter against her closed window. Thunder rumbled in the distance. If the silence was somehow tied to thunder and lightning she was screwed. There was no way she was going to experiment with electricity. She thought about the alley and how something had been able to block

142

everything out so effortlessly. Could she replicate that herself? Emma decided it was worth finding out as sleep threatened to take her. And what about Mattox? Was he projecting himself as a void in space or had she done that somehow? Sunday her dad would go to work and she could at least investigate the alley, but for now exhaustion won and everything faded to black.

In her dreamscape, the sun was setting as Emma soared like a bird just above the water's surface. The sun's purple and orange streamers were a feast to her eyes and its glow warmed her skin. As she glided she let the salt spray hit her tongue and energize her wings as they carried her towards the Cliffs of Moher. The steep jagged rocks jutted straight out of the crashing waves and beckoned her to climb them. She plunged deep into the water and emerged like a rocket up and over the cliff's ledge to pastures of green rolling hills. Driven to continue Southeast, Emma flew towards the ancient land that called to her.

Vehicles and roads faded, transforming into dirt trails and men on horseback the closer she got to Cadbury. A large tree lined hillfort stood vigil over the lush English countryside and welcomed her. Emma blinked and with a shimmer the empty hill transformed into a vibrant stone castle. Suddenly the hillfort turned dark and leather wings beat at the night sky as large masses screeched through the air. Trees around the castle creaked as ice leached into them, cracking them from the inside. The deafening whipping sound the wood made as it broke and exploded shrouded the screams coming from the castle as tree after tree fell. Defending their leader, knights surrounded their king who wielded a magnificent sword of golden light. Its light shimmered off a wall of encroaching black smoke. Emma gasped when she realized what the wall was. Hundreds of shadow creatures from her nightmares surrounded the hillfort. Dragons blacked out the remnants of the sun as they soared through the air circling the castle and demolishing it to rubble. A giant among men emerged from the wall of shadows and bowled down hundreds of knights as he made his way to the king. His tattered fluidic armor trailed behind him along with his most obedient beasts. With a simple flick of his wrist another wave of knights fell to their deaths. The giant stepped over ashen husks that once were men and cackled with pleasure.

Wind from dozens of dragon wings lifted the human dust into the air and the fallen men were reduced to unrecognizable mounds of grey powder. With every step

144

the giant's once emaciated skeletal form grew stronger, engorged with life essence from the fallen knights. He looked to the king and screeched and howled. The king showed no fear as he sliced through shadow beasts one after the other. Somehow, his remaining knights created purple glowing orbs out of midair that grew and encased the beasts banishing them back to their own realm.

The scene shimmered again and sounds of a celebration rang in Emma's ears. Children laughed and maidens giggled as everyone danced. The withered and dying trees were lush and green and the castle was no longer in ruins. Emma wondered if she was seeing something before or after the horrific battle she had just witnessed. *Before. Definitely before*, she thought, opening her senses up to the people below her. The king looked into the sky. Had he had heard her thoughts? Did he feel her presence when she listened to the court's emotions?

Come to us, Emma, you are one of us, the king's words bounced around in her skull as he stared at her floating there in the morning sky.

Emma's vision zoomed in to the king's table as a woman sat down. *Mom!* But the woman never looked Emma's way. She was focused on a young man sitting beside her. *Mattox?* At the mention of his name Mattox looked up at Emma.

You're one of us, Mattox stated inside Emma's head.

"You're one of us. You're one of us," the crowd chanted. Emma's mother finally looked up into the sky and smiled at her daughter.

"Mom!"

"Emm-" her mother's voice was cut off. Headlights rushed passed Emma's vision followed by a loud crash. Emma was thrust inside the car with her mother as it flipped over. Their bodies flew up and out of their seats crashing into everything over and over again as the car rolled. Windows shattered, metal crumpled, and the rolling finally stopped. A deathly silence shrouded the wreckage that had been their car. Pieces of glass clung to the blood and sweat coating her mother's skin and a river of her blood was pooling below their feet.

"Mom!" Emma gasped. The impact of the crash had left her breathless. "Don't leave me!"

Emma opened her eyes, covered her head with her pillow and wept. She hadn't been with her mom the night she died but the dream had been so real. Staying strong for her dad, she hadn't realized how much she missed her mother until she saw her and was ripped away from her even if it had been a nightmare.

The noises of the real world began to creep in along with other people's emotions. Someone in two apartments down was happy and celebrating a birthday. Not being alone with her grief and able to mourn her mother without someone's happiness flooding into her, Emma bit down on her pillow and screamed.

The empty soup can clanked and skipped as it hit the brick wall and rolled with an uneven lilt deeper into the alley. Emma pinched her arm. *Ow! Okay, I'm awake.* She kicked the dented can again as hard as she could and looked all around, hoping to stir...something. But the sun was shining straight down and without a cloud in the sky the dingy alley was void of most its shadows. *There's nothing here.* Emma rubbed her eyes and exhaled in frustration, *maybe I was just sleep deprived?* Defeated, and

147

only partially relieved, she headed home to await Monday and the second part of her investigation.

Slithering through the darkest crevices of the alley the creature stalked its prey. This one was worth a hefty bounty to the master, so ripe with overflowing life essence, the shadowy beast had never tasted anything quite like her. It shuddered, anticipating the opiate caresses its master would bestow upon it once it returned to the Netherworld. The earth's darkness would camouflage it soon and allow for more movement and better feeding ground. It sensed no guardians near and for that it was thankful. Being banished by a hunter now before devouring the sweet girl would undoubtedly be a death sentence at its master's hand. No, the creature would lie in wait near the girl. She seemed to be curious and it knew she would return. Knowing the girl's desires the creature set its lure and let a tangible thought be carried on the wind along with her name. *Emma.*

The bell rang and the cacophony of students shuffling out of class was drowning out Mr. Grey, "Don't forget I need your permission slips tomorrow for the field trip!"

Emma shook her head and put her earbuds in. A field trip with half the high school was not her idea of fun. She moaned at the thought of being trapped on a school bus the size of a sardine can with dozens of teenagers' emotions invading her mind. *Ugh! I hate my life!* Then her heart unexpectedly did a little flip flop as Mattox smiled at her before disappearing around the corner.

It wasn't until lunchtime Emma realized Mel was home with the flu. Mel texted Emma to save her a seat next to Mattox for when she got back unless they got married by then. Emma was responding with a sarcastic *"Ha ha"* when someone sat down across from her; someone with no emotional signature.

"Assume much?" Emma stated only half-heartedly as she looked up,

"Out of U and me," Mattox retorted.

"Ha, ha."

"Hey, I'm just following your lead," he beamed.

"I don't dance." Emma ranted.

"No? Because you're quite good at it from where I'm standing. Well, sitting actually, finally." A sly smile was plastered across his face.

He had her so distracted that for the second time since meeting Mattox Daniels everyone around them faded away. She looked from one side of the courtyard to the other with a smile on her face. Her grin widened as she turned back to Mattox, but the echoes soon returned.

"What?" he quizzed her.

"Nothing."

RADIOACTIVE RECKONING

"The painted lines on the floor are for your protection, as well as to ensure the integrity of our facility. Please stay behind the yellow line at all times during our tour. Go beyond it into the red zone without the proper identification and well," the tour guide in the white lab coat stepped over the line to demonstrate. An alarm sounded, followed by an influx of some serious looking men with severe haircuts. He quickly passed his key card over the line of demarcation and the alarm stopped. The guide waived at the security team. "As always, gentlemen, you have impeccable timing. Thank you." He turned back to his audience, "Now, if you'll follow me I'll show you one of our labs in action. This area behind the glass is a contaminant free zone or what you would call a clean room. Here at the Vaughn Institute we utilizes the same standards as NASA in our labs. The test tubes you see there..." the man in the lab coat droned on. Emma tried to concentrate on his words, but the close proximity to four classes of high schoolers was making it impossible.

Emma covertly sent a text to the flu ridden Mel. 'This sucks! U suck! Wish you were here.'

Seconds later Mel responded back. 'Lol, miss you too, biotch.'

Everything at the Vaughn Institute was crisp white and sterile except for the floor.   A wide band of green strategically flowed down the hallways lined on either side by a stripe of yellow and then red. Emma giggled, picturing herself on the yellow brick road to Oz. Only this Oz had been taken over by a demented clown and his crazy use of colors.

"Now, if you'll follow me, we'll make our way to the outer gardens and arboretum. Then we'll make our way into the hydroponics hangar and greenhouse." Emma let the tour guide's voice fade as she allowed students to pass her. She wanted to be in back of the crowd, reducing the amount of white noise in her head.

Since Mel was absent, Emma was feeling more isolated than usual with this field trip. She hadn't seen

Mattox at school, either. She nearly screamed out when an unexpected presence stood next to her.

"Well, this is where I'd come during the zombie apocalypse," Mattox chuckled as he matched Emma's pace in the crowd.

She had to laugh, "Why?"

"You mean besides the fact that it's built like Fort Knox? Let's see," Mattox counted things off with his fingers. "Self-sustaining food source, power source, and water supply. Don't even get me started on the labs. I mean, they could probably cure the zombies *and* create them," he chuckled again.

"Yeah, that lab made me feel like Peter Parker fixing to get bit by a radioactive spider or something."

"Are your Spidey senses tingling?" Mattox teased.

"Ha! All the time. Is the Vaughn Institute the same Vaughn as your building?" Emma asked.

"You never know." Mattox smirked.

Emma rolled her eyes. "Come on, I want to get outside, these hallways are making me claustrophobic and deathly afraid of clowns at the moment."

Mattox laughed, "After you, Spidey."

Emma took a deep breath enjoying the open air and shade from the beautiful boulevard of trees lining their path to the hydroponics facility. The white noise radiating from everyone had diminished outside, but they still muffled the beauty of the institute's grounds. Mattox stood facing her and smiled. He seemed to be enjoying her reaction to their surroundings. Just then Emma's teeth were rattled as someone shoved her from behind, and straight into Mattox.

"Hey, watch it!" Emma shouted as she was flung forward, reaching out trying not to fall.

Two boys ran by as Emma grabbed Mattox's forearms for balance.

"Sorry," they said in unison, but instead of sensing their remorse, the echoes in Emma's head became silent, almost as if they were being shielded.

Emma looked around in awe as she clung to Mattox's arms. She listened to the nature all around her. The birds were chirping, the leaves in the trees were rattling in the wind, and her classmates were simply talking all around her instead of inside her head. She looked at Mattox who was staring at her again and smiling.

He leaned over and softly whispered in her ear, "Who's the mysterious one now?"

Instinctively she stepped away from him as if his words had shocked her. As soon as she dropped his arms the noises returned. All of them. Slowly, as an experiment, she grabbed onto his arms again. He didn't protest, instead he held on to her as well. His grasp was strong and his hands were larger than she had realized. She felt small and safe in his embrace. And again the empathetic sounds ceased. Confused by the sudden quietness she looked around. Somehow touching Mattox had cloaked the echoes. Her mind had become deaf to everyone's emotions and it was beautiful. She could hear the birds chirping in the trees, children laughing as they played, and the sweet smell of cut grass and blooming jasmine as the wind threatened to sweep her off her feet.

Emma looked up at him, her eyes searching his, "How did you-" she stopped herself, not sure how much of her craziness she wanted to share. Her heart was pounding again and her mind was racing. Half of her frenzied response was from the realization that another human had the power to silence the voices in her head. The other half of her reaction was from Mattox himself.

"What's got you so worked up?" he asked, but to Emma he didn't seem that surprised.

Emma shook her head and dropped his arms, "I don't even know you."

Mattox nodded in agreement, put his hands in his pockets and started to walk away. Ten feet ahead of Emma, he stopped and turned. Mattox raised one of his hands and looked at it before holding it out to her, "Then get to know me."…

OTHER BOOKS BY CK DAWN

A Neophyte's Tale: A Netherwalker Short Story
(Netherwalker Series Prequel)

Cloak of Shadows (Netherwalker Series, Book 1)

Cloak of Echoes (Netherwalker Short Story, Book 1.5)

Cloak of Secrets (The Netherwalker Series, Book 2)
coming soon!

If you love my books, pretty please with Mr. Hunkie on top, consider leaving a review. Even just one sentence or two world mean the world!

You don't know who my sexy knight Mr. Hunkie is?

(That's right, he's a knight!)

Find out more at www.ckdawn.com

Thanks for reading! ~ ck